Change of Heart

CHANGE OF HEART

BARBARA ANDERSON

ISIS
LARGE PRINT
Oxford

First published in Great Britain 2004
by
Jonathan Cape, one of the publishers in
The Random House Group Ltd

Published in Large Print 2005 by ISIS Publishing Ltd,
7 Centremead, Osney Mead, Oxford OX2 0ES
by arrangement with
The Random House Group Ltd

British Library Cataloguing in Publication Data
Anderson, Barbara, 1926–
    Change of heart. – Large print ed.
    1. Older men – Fiction
    2. Large type books
    I. Title
    823.9'14 [F]

ISBN 0–7531–7283–6 (hb)
ISBN 0–7531–7284–4 (pb)

Printed and bound by Antony Rowe, Chippenham

IN MEMORY
J.A.W. – C.G.R.W.

Our planet
        is poorly equipped
                for delight.
One must
        snatch
           gladness
                from the days that are.
In this life
        it's not difficult to die.
To make life
        is more difficult by far.

Vladimir Mayakovsky,
'To Sergei Yessenin' 1928

CHAPTER
ONE

Heaven knows how it will end, but I will start with the house where I was born and the little window where the sun came peeping in at morn, which is a steal from a second-rate poem. I know it is second-rate because my father, who was well educated, told me so. He compared it with another poem which begins *Oft in the stilly night ere slumber's chain hath bound me* which is first rate. Something to do with sentiment rather than sentimentality perhaps, but I liked the idea of the sun peeping in the low windows of Cornwallis. Hardly have to get up — the sun, I mean.

My father described the small country town as "unique", which is Latin for one horse. Nevertheless it possessed a slow charm, the place where I was born; old trees, endless cows, a good view of the mountain when visible, and a band rotunda. Always a good sign, a band rotunda, redolent of community spirit and oompah and children tumbling about on good green grass.

I was born at home and, according to hearsay, arrived with a hiss and roar. "Only ten minutes old that noise, Mr Perkins," said the midwife to my father when he was allowed in to inspect. "Hard to believe, isn't it?"

1

She also said that I had no neck, head straight on my shoulders just like my mother. This was a joke, I learned later. There was nothing unusual about my mother's neck. I do remember, however, that she couldn't wear yellow.

There is something faintly unreliable about the word hearsay. A sense of information heard on the wing, rather than delivered face to face, sneezer to breather and eye to eye.

When my mother had recovered from my arrival she took me for short walks around the little town. One day the pram and I came to grief on some steps, an accident my father described as a triumph of enterprise over environment, there being few steps in flat Cornwallis. He added that he would have thought the town must be one of the safest places in the world for a little light carriage exercise but that a determined woman could achieve anything.

I bear the scar to this day, though you would have to look for it, as it is obscured by my moustache which I have worn for as long as it has been available. I have always been partial to moustaches. Mine is adequate but not grotesque, certainly not toothbrush. The French have a saying, *A kiss without a moustache is like an egg without salt*. A nice analogy, though one at which my wife Hester has ceased to smile.

My earliest true memory is my reaction to the sight of my first corpse when our neighbour, Miss Stratton, took me next door to see Mother before they took her away, because she looked so beautiful. I knew instantly that, beautiful or not, all was not well with the still

2

figure on the bed, and ran home howling, to be met by my mother and Mr Garland, a local gardener who sometimes gave her a hand with the heavy stuff. They were discussing the fate of a flowering currant, I remember. Mr Garland wouldn't give it house room: once they're a goner, they're a goner. My mother tucked me under one arm and said she would like to give it one more chance, and what on earth was the matter now with the Laird of Cockpen?

"She's dead, dead, dead like the squashed cat," I bawled.

"There, there," she said, patting vaguely. "Don't worry, Oliver, Mrs Stratton has gone to heaven. Nevertheless I'll speak to Miss Stratton, though perhaps not immediately. As I said Mr Garland, one more chance, please."

Despite the glimpse of mortality to which Miss Stratton had exposed me, she and I became allies. It was she who introduced me to the wonders of America and its language. She took me to the flicks. Unfortunately she insisted on holding my hand en route because of the responsibility, but it was worth it. Every Saturday morning we set off for what I learned to call the flea pit and she knew as the cinema. I don't remember my parents ever going to a film. If so, they never took me. It is thanks to Miss Stratton that I learned the joys of "Stick 'em up" and "Reach for the sky", of a land where gangsters said "Dees", "dem" and "dose guys" and swaggers were called bums, where anything could happen and often did, where words jumped with energy: a welcome change from Father's measured cadences.

My father, Charles Octavius Perkins, stood about my childhood like a large and distant tree. I see my mother, Amelia, more as a distracted-looking shrub. A white may perhaps — she certainly had the same peppery smell — but the connection may be subconscious. Her second name was May, but she preferred to be known as Amelia as who would not.

My mother described herself as romantic. She drifted, she dreamed, she disliked household tasks and took little naps. She also disliked a habit to which I was prone as a child. I made things up. Mr Sergeant the butcher's wooden leg was called Tiger because a tiger had bitten it off in Mandalay where the flying fishes play. Our teacher Miss Presley had a mad sister whom she locked in the garden shed each morning before she came to school. I had seen this alarming sight, I said, and described it in detail — the curled uncut fingernails, the hair, the wide wild eyes. Standard Four responded like eighteenth-century Bedlam viewers. The phantom Miss Presley and the leg called Tiger gave me a drawcard. Lonely children must find them where they can.

Frankie Boyd, the part-time assistant at the public baths, an amiable youth with pimples and enormous feet, was another victim. I told the class that Frankie peed in the baths. Owing to various lapses in the past they were less surprised than they might have been. "Pisser," we muttered as we handed over our sixpences. Eventually he leaned across the counter, grabbed my collar in one hand and Billy Bowland's in the other, and hissed, "Whad'y'a saying, y'dorks."

"Kisser!" I yelped.

"Yeah," gasped Billy, "Kisser Boyd — that's what the tarts call you."

Pisser, engulfed by a raspberry red tide of embarrassment and pleasure, dropped us. "Who? Which one?"

"All of them," we said.

"OK, get away in, y'toe rags."

It couldn't last, this power, this audience. The word was out; there were murmurs beneath the banner of the Mothers' Union. Sons were asked by mothers, had Mr Sergeant's leg been eaten by a tiger? No. Did Miss Presley have a potty sister in the back shed? No. So then, Olly Perkins told whoppers. Pisser was not mentioned. Pissing was rude, and boys learn early that the joys of rudery are lost on mothers.

I was surprised by my mother's concern. I was proud of my stories and had never thought of them as whoppers, let alone that they might be harmful. My mother never alluded to my inspired make-ups as such. She came out of her reverie (one of her favourite words) long enough to say I had been Romancing and must be careful, though she never said why. I gathered that she used the word to indicate exaggeration, picturesque visions of imagination, distorted memories. Whoppers in fact, in all but name.

Romance, memory, hearsay and whoppers. What more could a man need.

My only other drawcard with my contemporaries was my friendship with Barney Scott, the bike man. I was the first boy allowed to hang around, to mess about with bikes and Barney. Others followed. We cut patches. We disembowelled inner tubes from punctured tyres, soaked the collapsed grey guts in water to find the leak, then marked the spot with an indelible purple X before handing them over to Barney to glue the patch. Sometimes we sprinkled on the chalk to complete the job, but not often. Barney was a man's man; he made us welcome, never gave unnecessary advice and he explained the wonder of Sturmey-Archer gears. He showed us how to do each job and left us to it.

I wonder what happened to him. Death presumably. Must have by now.

Charles Octavius, as I said, was a man of presence, but lacking in what might be called clout. Clout would have been abhorrent to him. Money also was suspect and not to be mentioned on any account. My mother told me that Father was like the King of England; he did not carry money, had never been inside a butcher's shop, boiled an egg or changed a tyre.

He was born in a small village in Essex in 1876, the eighth of ten children born to the Reverend Henry Horatio Perkins and his wife, Blanche.

Like his father and his older brothers, Charles was destined to take Holy Orders and become a minister in the Anglican Church. The career choices for impecunious sons of clergymen were slim in late-Victorian times. The Church was one salvation for younger sons, commissions in the Army or Navy another; failing that, there were the colonies.

What else could they do, where could they go, those well-educated young men with pale hands and beautiful hair and little money.

Charles entered his university college in the nineties, taking with him the same pewter beer mug over which his elder brothers, Gurth, Egbert and Lionel, had held tenure during their time there. It is mine now, the mug, rather battered but with a nice patina.

As well as the beer mug my father and his brothers took with them something of far more value: their sure and certain belief in Almighty God. It lay within them, this truth; unseen, unmentioned, but there, glowing like a warm ember of comfort in times of melancholy or malaise or indeed joy. Father told me that when confronted by representations of the Sacred Heart in the establishments of his more Popish brethren he was filled with a sense of — how shall I put it? — empathy perhaps, for want of a better word. Not in a religious sense, God forbid, more in the positioning of this inner source of strength.

A classical scholar like his brothers, Charles had Latin and Greek and a fervent love and admiration of things Greek and Roman. As a youth he had seen the stadium at Delphi and the indentations in the stone where five thousand years before the birth of Christ Greek athletes had placed a foot for speedy take-off. These worn dips, he told me, his eyes damp with emotion, were the forerunners of modern starting blocks.

His special interest in Roman art was those astonishing painted burial masks from the second century AD. The only time I have seen an original was in New York. It was that of a middle-aged Egyptian woman with short greying hair and an impelling gaze from eyes heavily blackened with kohl. I found it both chilling and inspiring *because* it was so lively, so obviously a portrait of a real person. Father told me that originally, before the archaeologists and/or grave robbers removed the masks, these glowing portraits topped the mummified bodies of the deceased. Some of them, apparently, had been regarded as part of the family. Stood around the dining room, that sort of thing. *Memento mori* can be overdone, in my opinion, though of course we all have our preferences.

What a wonderful place New York is. I recommend New York most highly to anyone. It is the only place I have been to Abroad and the only one I should like to revisit. The place was booming, the people seemed to have mastered the art of being both busy and cheerful, and the unexpected happened anywhere, like the day we saw a black man walking along Broadway with a large snake coiling and recoiling about his shoulders. Hester asked him what species of snake it was, the man replied it was a *python* and went calmly on his way.

I was attending an international dental conference at the time. I had registered as soon as I saw it was to take place in New York, and Hester was in entire agreement. I remember little of the conference, possibly because I did not attend many sessions, but I do remember that the *python's* name was Jacko.

8

But I digress. Charles also had a small collection of reproduction Greek vases depicting, I discovered when I was high enough to reach for them, scenes reflecting not only the moods and attitudes of their day but also mythical scenes. One or two of these showed excited-looking satyrs chasing fleet-footed but seemingly untroubled maidens endlessly round terracotta curves.

What did I think of them? Not much at the time, but I should like to see them now. Such things give comfort to an older man, a sense of, shall we say, continuity. We can be tempted by the thought that there is not much point in the world continuing to roll once we have, as it were, shoved off, but this is a solipsistic thought and should not be mentioned except when we sit with friends in what my father used to call unbuttoned ease. When we talk the sun down, thrash out the things that matter, the eternal verities of life and death and how to cope with both or either. I have had two friends in my time. A few more would have been welcome but one must be thankful for what one gets in the way of friends, or wives. Or children.

I first became aware of the rest of the world's probable lack of interest in my future demise not from Mrs Stratton's death, nor indeed from that of the cat, but many years later when I returned to collect my mail from one of the hospitals in which I had almost died. The administration had been slow in forwarding it, and mail is important to a man of intellectual curiosity. After all something agreeable might glint from the tailings of bills, brochures and requests for charity

9

(*Your stamp is an extra gift*), even if it is only a Special on precooked sausages.

Be that as it may, the mail handed over the desk to me that day was disappointing: a Get Well card from Miss de Lillo, my surgery nurse, depicting a white-coated Rabbit House Surgeon with a stethoscope around his neck examining a large anonymous stomach and saying cheerfully to the attendant Rabbit Nurse, "We've got a biggie here, Trixie." Plus a power bill.

My point, however, is not the quality of my mail, but my sharp feeling of surprise. I had left the ward, or rather been pushed out of it, more dead than alive, certainly, but definitely out, and yet nothing had changed. The overcrowded ward, the clanging food trolleys, the busy corridors, all were exactly the same. The inhabitants, professional, prone, wheelchaired or ambulatory, continued about their respective businesses without a glance. I didn't expect them to care, of course, but I hadn't, for some reason, expected total invisibility. White-out.

Death is inevitable, of course, and not to be sneezed at if the moment is right. I was not dead obviously. I was standing at the desk clutching my Get Well rabbits and the power bill but I realised, and this is the important point, *I might just as well have been.*

I was tempted to make a small gesture, some light-hearted reference to the fact that they could all go home now that I was no longer in need of their services (or not so much), but I refrained due to wisdom culled many years ago when I undertook physiotherapy. I lay prone on the treatment slab as the operator, I can call him nothing else, began pummelling my back with such force that I had to remind him this was not some hack beneath his hands but me, and would he please take care. I mentioned this politely with a slight whimsical smile. The young man said nothing, but both his breathing and his thumping hands became heavier. I learned a lesson. When you are in someone else's hands it is best to lie low and avoid comment, especially when the hands are those of the medical fraternity and their ancillaries. These are busy people, these healers and choppers, and not given to quips — except for that smirk of self-satisfaction when their initial diagnosis of one's lumps and bumps has been confirmed by further investigation (see Rabbit with stethoscope).

But at least we can remain interested. Why should we not be interested in our own demise. Apart from the fact that we have no way of knowing after the event, why should we not be surprised that planets continue to spin, trolleys to clang and dogs to bark when one has ceased to be? My son Copland says, quite often, "Whose life is it anyway?" Surely death is of equal interest from, shall we say, a personal point of view.

But back to Charles Octavius. Have I mentioned that his career was varied, surprisingly so considering that, like his brothers Gurth, Egbert and Lionel, he had always been a conscientious and devout student of theology.

He told me in later life of an experience he had had at a religious retreat. He had missed a train connection and arrived late. As he walked up the long drive towards the chapel, the still silence of the morning was broken by strong male voices lifted in praise.

> *Immortal, invisible, God only wise*
> *In light inaccessible hid from our eyes . . .*
> *Oh Lord we would render*
> *Oh help us to see*
> *'Tis only the splendour of light hideth thee.*

"I was stunned by the glory and the truth and the wonder," he said. "I fell on my benders on the damp grass and gave thanks."

Until, that is, he tangled with the Thirty-Nine Articles. They are not a statement of Christian doctrine, these Articles, more short summaries which seek to define the Anglican position vis-à-vis medieval doctrinal corruptions among Roman Catholics or Calvinists. Article 28, for example, is concerned with that old stumbling block, transubstantiation. Article 6 states that holy scripture contains all that is necessary for salvation. Article 21 that General Councils are not of themselves infallible. Whereas Article 17 contains masterly ambiguity about the difficult topic of predestination.

Before 1865, aspiring postulates to the Anglican clergy had to swear their allegiance to each one of the Thirty-Nine Articles. By the time of Father's ordination, however, he would have been required only to affirm that the Articles were "agreeable to the Word of God" and undertake not to teach in contradiction of them.

So why could this pious young man stumble over something as toothless as the veracity of the Thirty-Nine Articles? He told me himself that he had never been one of those haunted young Victorian men who felt their immortal souls to be at risk if they wrestled with the conundrums raised by Darwin in *On the Origin of Species by Means of Natural Selection* and, even more alarming, *The Descent of Man*.

Like St Augustine of Hippo, my father believed in the essential goodness of all creation. Or had done so, until this belief was shaken when he spent his holidays assisting an exhausted old priest working among the wretchedly poor in the East End of London. This experience, said Charles, seared him for life. Evil, for both St Augustine and Father, was the privation of some good which ought to be had. This privation for those half-starving in the slums was patently obvious; what's more, evil on such a vast scale existed within less than a hundred miles of the Essex village where Henry preached his sermons in the Saxon church with the remains of a Dane's skin pinned above the door, and where his mother Blanche and unmarried sister Decima visited the rural sick.

His experience of life in the slums damaged Charles, not because of the nature of the work but the endless frustrations involved when he realised he could do so little.

"That and the particular Thirty-Ninth Article," he said. "I realised I must give up my vocation as an ordained priest."

I am surprised, with hindsight, that I never asked with which one of the Articles he could not be doing. I have a nodding acquaintance with a few of them but I have never checked, nor in fact made a wobbly guess as to which one he might have been alluding. Odd really.

Henry accepted with sorrow his son's decision not to be ordained, as did Gurth and Egbert, but Lionel was a horse of a different temper. Obviously, he said, Charles had been put off by the thought that he might end up being a perpetual curate in an East End parish. "I shouldn't worry, Chas," he said, "I'm sure the Almighty would not be so unkind."

Not unnaturally my father took offence at this slander and the rift continued. Charles never mentioned his brother Lionel. If I asked after him he would say only that Lionel had not fulfilled his father's expectations. He had left the Church soon after Father, and died of disappointment in the West Indies. My mother said no one can die of disappointment. Disappointment is a condition not a disease. Men might die disappointed, certainly, as many of us probably will, but not from disappointment, in the West Indies or anywhere else. And had anyone seen her reading glasses — ah, there they were.

After his decision Charles changed his college and began reading Law. Fortunately he was able to obtain what my son Copland calls "cross credits" for some of his theological studies, as a result of which he did not have to begin reading Law from scratch. The worst, he said, undeniably the most sullen and numbing subject of all, was Torts. "Never, dear boy, read Torts."

He found the subject of Law boring after the intellectual cut and thrust of Theology, especially as the nineties had been a particularly interesting time in the annals of the Anglican Church. All, all were there, he said. Doubt, schism, fervour, the glorious and the banal. I suggested that perhaps the mixture had always been similar, not only for the Anglican Church but for all living faiths, but Charles denied this vehemently.

He came down from Oxford with a good Second and the realisation that he would not only have to practise law but, furthermore, he would have to pull himself up by his own bootstraps. There would be no friendly word, much less preferment from relations or friends of his father, all of whom were clerical to the core.

About this time he married my mother, Amelia May Trancer, the daughter of a colleague of his father's whose vicarage lay within walking distance. My mother, despite, or perhaps because she considered herself a romantic, had good sense and a will of iron.

"If you hate law, Chas," she said, "why do it? Why don't we go to Queensland and grow pineapples with Bobby."

Which they did, with disastrous results. Bobby, Amelia's brother, was both feckless and useless; what little money my parents had been able to save ran out; the pineapples were sickly and the droughts long. "Never live in Queensland, Oliver, a ghaster of a place, believe me."

They struggled on for five years watching the crop fail year after year. Drought — real, seemingly endless drought — is the cruelest card nature can play. It is so slow in its devastation, so bitter in its results. Crops, stock and human hope die by inches. No wonder the aboriginals had rain dances.

My mother, once again, made the decision. Bobby and nature had both failed them, also Bobby was showing signs of going bush. The pineapples were neglected, there was drink, there were women, there was talk. It was simply not good enough. Amelia would buy tickets to New Zealand with the money her mother had given her for a rainy day. They would find a small farm near Auckland. *"There are no droughts at Pokeno,"* wrote her school friend Bessie, who lived nearby in Auckland, a city spoken well of by Rudyard Kipling. *Last, loveliest, exquisite, apart.* You couldn't use any of those words for Colchester, much less Brisbane in those days.

There were no droughts at Pokeno but there was clay. Clay swallowed your shoes, damn near sunk your gumboots, impeded each step in winter with khaki clods of mud which dried to khaki dust in summer. The soil was sour, the work backbreaking, the cows foul-tempered and the bull worse. "Clay's clahy stuff," said the hired help and disappeared within a month.

"I think, Charles," said my mother eventually, "that you might have to practise law again. Perhaps," she said, sluicing a clod from her gumboot with the so-called garden hose, "it might not be so bad here. We could go somewhere small. Taranaki, perhaps. There is a mountain there, is there not? That would be nice. I should like a mountain to lift up mine eyes unto. It's time we had things easier. After all we've been married for ten years."

As usual Amelia was right. My father put up his brass plate on a corner block in Cornwallis — *Charles G. Perkins B.A. LL.B.* — and life went on.

I, Oliver Gurth Perkins, was born soon after. My mother chose my first name; she had always had a soft spot for Cromwell, and Gurth was my father's favourite brother.

My father was fifty at the time, my mother over forty. I saw and still do see myself as having been an only child of ageing parents, like the harrowing death notices which my mother kept during the war and showed me later. *Only son of widowed mother*, for example. It was the "only" which made it so harrowing, the "o" in it.

"Look at them," she said, "woe, moan, groan, it is always the 'o' that does it."

Her favourite poet was Edgar Allan Poe.

CHAPTER
TWO

Have I mentioned why I have started this journal? It is not so much my wish to relate or reveal my family history, and certainly not to attempt catharsis. God forbid that I should let it all hang out. I know what has happened in the past and I don't imagine my family would be interested, but I have to have something to do, you see, in case someone slips past Miss de Lillo at the reception desk and appears in my surgery unexpectedly. It must be something involving pen and paper, something mildly intellectual in appearance, which can be slipped in the top drawer of my desk at any time. One doesn't want to be caught napping.

Miss de Lillo, my receptionist-cum-dental nurse, is not a problem in this regard. Not only is she aware of my need for cryptic crosswords but she is quite used to seeing me asleep in my dental chair, which, when out to its full extension, I have found to be the most comfortable couch in the world for a siesta. I am rather proud of my chair. It is the state-of-the-art dental chair, an all-singing, all-dancing Planmeca Prostyle, upholstered in a rather attractive shade of shiny blue plastic. I bought it a few years ago. My old wooden-armed chair had to go. Even I could see that and my wife Hester insisted. Suffering discomfort in a dentist's *chair*, she said, is wanton cruelty. I am glad I took her advice.

I have not liked to enquire as to where Miss de Lillo takes her siesta. I fancy perhaps on the sofa in the waiting room. The screen by the front door would give her a few moments' grace if disturbed.

Be that as it may, the keeping of my journal has been forced upon me by the most infuriating circumstances. Not one of the nearby booksellers now carries, as they say, paperback collections of cryptic crosswords from the major English newspapers. No *Times*, no *Daily Telegraph* — I need not go on. I have complained most strongly in each shop, but the answer has always been the same. They could order them in for me if I like, from the suppliers in Auckland, but there is little call for them nowadays. And me on my knees before them.

But, you may say, you could import them from their source.

This action was recommended to me by a helpful young assistant with a couple of inches of tanned midriff visible behind the counter of Books 'n' That. I thanked her, but for some reason this solution sticks in my craw. Why should I import them? These essential adjuncts to a civilised man's life have been dropped, spurned, excluded from the very market that needs them most.

And besides, the cost would be prohibitive.

There are other alternatives certainly. I read widely and with pleasure but the problem is I find myself unable to read all day, even if I have several books on the go. Nor can my needs be met by the lesser breed of cryptic, let alone noncryptic or, worse, anagrams. The secret of my need for this particular subspecies lies in the fact that solving a good cryptic crossword can give one a quick sting of intellectual achievement and, even better, happiness. One is using one's wits, and it can make one feel, or pretend to feel, the muscles of the brain being stretched. Lateral thinking is required, a sound mind in a seated body. The secret joy, the gleam of what I can only call bliss when one realises that the clue *Soldier ant's remark to a friend* (7 across, 7 letters) is *Passant*.

I believe that this glimpse of light sometimes given to the human mind is one of the wonders of the world. Einstein described it as a tingle at the fingertips, a physiological insight, and he should know.

Good heavens, this is wonderful. I have been typing away on my ancient Olivetti since nine this morning and time has flown; wingèd chariots, I assure you. Why did I never think of a journal before. Definitely the answer, or one of them. No interruptions except for the welcome one at 11 a.m. of Miss de Lillo bearing what she calls my NATO Standard, an expression she acquired from a cousin who worked in Hawaii during the 1970s. A NATO Standard, Miss de Lillo never forgets to mention, is a cup of coffee with milk but no sugar, as favoured by the majority of Americans working in the North Atlantic Treaty Organisation in Brussels.

Miss de Lillo was very fond of this cousin until he sent her what she called a Dear John letter advising her that he no longer loved her. I attempted commiseration but she would have none of it. "Where on earth would I fit him in now," she said.

She is undoubtedly busy. There is never a film unseen, a play ignored, a sick friend unvisited. She is an excellent woman and I bless her cousin's stupidity. She is also attractive in a rangy, messy sort of way. I am very fond of her.

Something strikes me. "Miss de Lillo, don't we have a patient this afternoon?"

"Yes, Mr Perkins. Mrs Stubbs. But not till 2p.m."

Excellent. Time for a leisurely slice of focaccia and a rather nasty cappuccino or perhaps tea at The Tulip next door, a siesta on the chair with *The Ingoldsby Legends*, one of my father's favourites which I have another go at from time to time, then Mrs Stubbs and her partial plate, followed by another quick cup and a vanilla melting moment, and it will almost be time to walk home.

As I glanced at the pile of typed sheets beside me, however, I felt rather startled. I realised I have been writing all this time and have scarcely mentioned my own family: my wife Hester and my son Copland. Like drowned unweighted bodies they have been waiting to surface when their time is ripe.

There is of course no need to mention them. As I have said before, I already know them. However, if I am to continue this journal it seems churlish to have spent so much time on my parents and none on my more immediate family.

On leaving New Plymouth Boys' High School I tried primary school teaching but fled in terror after a few years. One of the things I most disliked was the smell of the primers' room, especially in winter; that melded stench of hot wool, chalk dust and occasional little accidents gave me the willies.

After my abortive teaching career I volunteered for the New Zealand Army but was turned down. Flat feet. I don't know why this condition is always considered mildly comic, but then so are false teeth and bandy legs and cuckoldry.

Schadenfreude, I suppose. All are part of the human condition, after all. Like Pisser Boyd's pimples which Father called grogblossoms when situated on the nose. Which reminds me of one of Copland's early favourites:

> *ASK your Mother for sixpence*
> *To see the big giraffe,*
> *He's whiskers on his pimples*
> *And pimples on his*
> *ASK your mother etc.*

Not the stuff for an ex-clergyman's son's repertoire but his glee was worth it at the time.

I had considered studying Medicine originally but the thought of all those patients, row after row of them flat on their backs with plastic bags yellowing as the tide rose, and drips and blood everywhere. No. Anything was preferable. Besides, the Medical course was longer and I was already a late starter. Dentistry it was.

I had trouble passing the examinations, which naturally held me up as well. I could be said to have limped my way through my BDS. I also disliked the practical. The "Open Wide" side of Dentistry did not appeal either.

My dislike of exams surprised Charles Octavius. He told me dispiriting stories of his infallible system of passing each and every exam he had ever sat. How he had always stopped studying at least a week before finals. Golf, he said, golf was the answer. In some mysterious and to my mind unlikely way, daily games of golf settled the store of knowledge inside his large bushy head so that it welled out in streams the moment he opened the examination papers. He had enjoyed exams immensely, great fun.

He told me this not in anger but in wistful incomprehension. And why had I chosen Dentistry of all things when all I could do was English? Even my Latin was disappointing and they didn't teach Greek. Perhaps, he said sadly, the classical strain was running out.

The Dentistry School in Dunedin was a grisly place in those days, a large grim-looking brick building situated in the centre of town. I firmly believed then and still do that the dental nurse's main duty was to hold the patients down. I forget exactly how many chairs lined each side of the Main Hall, each with a dental trainee, an attendant nurse and patient. The noise from the twenty or so foot-pedal drills plus the cries of anguished children is with me still.

The standard of beauty in the intake of dental nurses in my final year was higher than usual and the prettiest of all was Hester Hope. She was small and quick, bright eyed and kind to the patients — not necessarily a feature of Main Hall student nurses, although I hesitate to mention it. "Rinse please," from a busty dragon had the sibilant hiss of a rifle bullet. Drunk with power, I suppose, or alternatively *The bleating of the kid excites the tiger*. No, not a merry sight, Main Hall in those days.

But Hester, ah Hester. The first time I asked her to accompany me to the pictures on Saturday night she was wearing what she called my yellow tam. To me it was a halo encircling her crisp dark hair.

I still cannot understand why she said "Yes" to me that night, and for many following Saturdays. Nor, I discovered, did most of the rest of my year. I heard Talbot and Jackson at the urinal one day, heard my name and that unattractive tone of voice, and instinctively ducked into the shelter of a stall, for which I was grateful later.

Talbot spoke first. "You know that gormless twit Perkins is going out with Nurse Hope?"

Going out with. The phrase can still raise minor frissons. Going out with was a first step, a sort of Learner's Licence for wrestling with the girl of your choice in the back seats of the cinema. Or in any other dark shelter one could find, which was not easy in Dunedin in those days. None of the students had cars, and motorbikes were few, as well as being ill designed for the purpose in hand.

A zipper ripped. "You're kidding," said Jackson.

"Betty told me and she'd know. Mad about him, she says."

"But Christ — Nurse Hope and *Perkins*."

"Yeah, Perkins."

I asked Hester. "Why do you love me?"

She laughed. She often laughed at things I said. She undid the plaited leather button of my jacket and snuggled against my Fair Isle jersey.

"Because you're so sweet. And funny. You make me laugh. And I love the way your hair grows. No, truly."

It was not exactly what I had hoped to hear, but it served.

Sod Talbot and Jackson, I thought, and have had no reason since to change my mind. Both have probably died of disappointment in the West Indies by now. Or so I hope.

The day after I graduated, Hester and I were married in the Dunedin Registry Office, an eerie business with a sad-eyed Registrar who looked as though he was going to burst into scalding tears at any moment. The witness was my friend Alexander Rivers, a more amiable dental student. Alex was one of the two friends I have mentioned. He died in the Tangiwai train disaster in 1953 when the young Queen was here and banner signs on the local freezing works cried *Haere mai te Queenie*. Irreplaceable, a completely irreplaceable man — wife and two small children — but there you are. It was a sad time.

Hester and I were pleased with ourselves and our visit to the Registrar. I had told her about St Paul's advice that it was better to marry than burn and she agreed wholeheartedly.

Her parents were appalled. They behaved as though we had been married in a brothel.

My parents, to my relief, remained calm. Father said that God's presence can be felt in a Registry Office just as well as Westminster Abbey. "*Consider the lilies of the field*," he said, adding that we might perhaps have asked them to be present though of course they wouldn't have been able to come. "Balclutha," he continued, "away down there? Does she have a southern burr? People go on about it so, but I've never been convinced that such a thing exists. Have you given any thought as to what you're going to live on?" Amelia said she was disappointed not to be present, but on the other hand it had saved her having to hunt for a hat and we were welcome in Cornwallis any time.

We went immediately. Where else could we go. As Charles had noticed, we had no money.

Charles loved Hester on sight. His comments, however, had a whiff of the Talbot and Jacksons. I heard him asking her one day why she had married me, which I thought rather odd. I became his daughter-in-law's husband, a role which I admit suited me well. Hester's arrival had, how shall I say, taken some of the heat from the searchlight he used to examine the disappointing phenomenon of his only child.

26

Amelia said Hester had pretty hair and would she like two chops or one this evening, as she, the cook, had not yet been to the butcher.

Hester asked for two.

"Two," said Amelia. "That makes seven then. Thank you."

The lines were drawn.

Hester told me as we heaved about in one of the sagging beds in the spare bedroom that she had felt at home in Cornwallis from the moment my father headed off the cream running down the George V coronation jug and muttered, "Not well designed. Like the man himself. All he did was stick in stamps and shoot things."

"Have you noticed," he said later as he handed me the hoe for the asparagus bed, "that Hester has a classical Grecian nose?"

"No."

"No? How extraordinary."

"You'll have to meet my family soon, Olly," said Hester as we greeted one other that night, rolling towards each other in the licensed grip of matrimony.

"Yes," I said.

Copland Gurth Perkins was born in Tawa where I was doing a locum for a man who for reasons of his own was circumnavigating the world in a small yacht. A nice place, Tawa, though we soon left. I was fortunate to find a practice to buy in town, one in the last stages of terminal decay and therefore affordable. We also found a rundown house in Thorndon in a convenient position near a primary school. There are not many capital cities where you can walk to work and I find the wind bracing and the libraries good. We called our son after both Charles Octavius's ancestral village in Essex and his favourite brother, a last-ditch attempt on my part to please my father although he was no longer with us.

Copland, or Copper, as he renamed himself in his first week of primary school, is about forty now and he has come home. His wife left him some time ago. It was not a happy marriage. In fact it lasted only six years before Corinne left him to live with her new lover Marty on the coast of Coromandel where the early pumpkins blow. Copper seemed calm about her departure but devastated at the loss of his four-year-old daughter, Poppy Esther. I think that was the beginning of his lack of interest in life, when *accidie* took over, when his, oh dear, his Coplandness began.

Hester and I shared his sorrow. Now I look forward to the school holidays when Poppy comes to stay almost as much as I did in my teaching days. We both do, though of course Hester is more involved.

As for her name, Poppy Esther Perkins, I did my best. I explained to her mother that Poppy Esther had an uneuphonious clang, that it sounded like a synthetic fabric, one of those byproducts from the refining of crude oil, but Corinne replied that she didn't give a stuff what I thought.

Copper is fed up with being a social worker with the Department of Social Welfare, now called WINZ, which stands for Work and Industry New Zealand. Copper is fed up with a lot of things. I suggested that he should write a letter to the paper delineating the first ten and sign it *Fed up of Thorndon* but he did not reply.

I think that clarifies my immediate family connections.

Now for Mrs Stubbs' partial plate. I should add that I don't do major Open Wide work now. I hand on to the young and hungry any procedures which require a high degree of manual dexterity or, in the case of extractions, physical strength. However, there are always simple fillings, or, more frequently among the age range of my patients, re-fillings, or the final solution of impressions and adjustments for dentures. I am good at dentures. Not the actual making of them of course but I ensure a good fit, insist on a reasonable colour and comfort for the wearer at all times. I intend to cut down a little more soon, but I hope to hang on to dentures.

Sometimes though not Oft in the stilly night, ere slumber's chain hath bound me, I wonder why people still come to be treated by a man of seventy-five. I can scarcely ask them, but Miss de Lillo has let drop that patients tell her they enjoy coming to Mr Perkins because he is so polite, always gives injections and does not overcharge. Also I am as meticulous as Miss de Lillo about cleanliness, offer comfortable seating in the waiting area, and carry a good range of magazines: a blend of gossip, preferably Royal, food, gardens and the dramas of Celebrities who Miss de Lillo tells me she has never heard of and why do they all look the same.

And there is always The Tulip next door for a rewarding chocolate vanilla slice after treatment. Calories after caries. I am all for it.

CHAPTER
THREE

Escorted by Miss de Lillo, Mrs Stubbs scuttled into the surgery. She was small and wiry with the bright-eyed gaze of the indomitable old. She had not let herself go, not for a moment. Scarlet lipstick slashed across the pleats of her powdered face, artificial red cherries bobbed from the bun hat above her grey coat and skirt.

Greetings were exchanged, queries as to our respective health reciprocated. Good, good. We were both delighted to hear so. I pulled on my disposable gloves, Miss de Lillo patted the seat of the blue reclining chair and Mrs Stubbs took a flying leap. The paper bib was clipped, I pressed the pedal. The patient lay horizontal and at ease.

She looked up into my eyes above the mask. "This chair is so comfy after the old one," she sighed. "Remember you asked me not to dig my nails into the arms. It would ruin the mahogany veneer, you said."

Mrs Stubbs, Miss de Lillo and I laughed as we have laughed each and every time we hear the story. I leaned forward. "The plate is giving you some trouble, I gather Mrs Stubbs?"

Mrs Stubbs' voice was crisp. "*Partial* plate."

"Yes, partial plate," I said, and sank slowly on to the black and white vinyl beside the chair.

I can remember the sound of the doll-sized magnifying mirror clattering from my hand as I spilled forward. After which, I knew no more.

Apparently the ensuing action went something like this. Mrs Stubbs scrambled down to kneel beside me and attempted to take my pulse, then remembered her watch had no second hand and she had forgotten what was normal anyway.

Miss de Lillo rang 111.

The ambulance arrived within minutes and the two young men were so efficient, so fit, so *there*. Smiling at them over the portable electrocardiogram machine, Steve suggested a cup of tea with sugar for the ladies later, to be drunk slowly for shock. He and Glen would never recommend it for a patient. The ladies had done the right thing, he said. So often people rush in, not to mention moving the victim.

Mrs Stubbs couldn't take her eyes off Glen's shaven head, so neat, like Yul Brynner. And so quick, but gentle with pulse, blood pressure, the portable machine as they attended to the patient now lying on his back with eyes shut. They say you go grey and you do. Grey-blue. Awful.

Steve pronounced it a Hospital case. "Something slightly irregular with the ECG. Give A & E a buzz, Glen, tell them we're on the way. He'll be right, ladies. No worries. Cup of tea with sugar, remember. And we'll need the next of kin. Wife is it? Ah, thanks. OK. Got your end, Glen? Bye, ladies."

And they were gone and the ladies were left staring at each other. It was as though a beacon had passed through the surgery, Miss de Lillo said, had flooded the scene with light and made all things clear and no secrets hid, then swung away again, leaving the muddle and confusion and fright behind.

She insisted on a taxi for Mrs Stubbs. "Mr Perkins would insist," she said and I would have, quite right too.

Normally Mrs Stubbs wouldn't have dreamt of it apparently. A muffin and a flat white next door and she would have been fine, but it was the non-adjusted partial plate. She couldn't chew properly and she just wanted to get home. Though heaven knows what she would do then. Take the plate out, yes, but then what. "Mr Perkins of all people," she kept murmuring.

Miss de Lillo said I would be all right.

Mrs Stubbs said yes, of course I would, but a tear fell on the snub-nosed toe of her lace-up, and they both stared at the bright splash not knowing what to say, what to hope for or how to part until Miss de Lillo remembered she hadn't rung Mrs Perkins and that would be Mrs Stubbs' taxi. Mrs Stubbs agreed and said could she ring her sometime, and would Miss de Lillo be here and Miss de Lillo said of course, where else would she be.

I grabbed the keys and ran to the car. It's odd the way you react. The newsreader's voice as I turned on the ignition with details of the latest murder, the victim's children being looked after by friends, the small town in shock, four trampers missing in the Kaimanawas, thousands dead in floods in Pakistan. Each item clear as a bell and the rest of life a haze. I was through the hospital gates before I remembered the Casualty Department had been moved last year. A new building, the Something Wing, a great asset and not before time, but where in heaven's name was it? The parking attendant waved me through, still shouting instructions as the bar lifted: out the gate, turn left, straight on till you see the signs, can't miss them.

The new building is impressive; the man at the Control Station glanced from his computer. Yes, Mr Perkins was being examined now. Yes, I could go through to him.

He lay with his bloodless mouth open and his eyes closed. His hands were terrifying, pale and still as death. My legs gave way, someone slid me a chair, people smiled, the ECG machine above his head continued tracing, the line across the screen blipped, dipped, carried on. People can read those things. It is probably quite simple.

His eyes opened. "Hullo Hester," he said. "How kind of you to come."

My hands tightened. He didn't mean the trite phrase, or not the way it sounded, so detached, po-faced. He can't do emotion. I have known this for ever. Why fuss now.

I could feel the stiffness of my smile. "Not at all."

"You're very tolerant," he murmured.

This frightened me more. He is the tolerant one: *They can't help it, We are all different, Let it pass.*

Occasionally I have wondered whether his acceptance of all humanity and their varying beliefs and what he might have called their un-*usual* behaviour is in fact tolerance, or merely lack of interest. The world and its millions concern him little. He doesn't do people. And why should he. Who makes the rules?

My eyes filled with hot gritty tears. What on earth was I doing? My trenchmate Olly in trouble and me sitting analysing his soul like some well-meaning clown with a ponytail and a degree in God knows what.

Olly. Please, Olly, it's me.

A petite young woman with round glasses and a tab reading *Dr Rowena Bilby* appeared. "You mustn't worry, Mrs Perkins. He looks much worse than he is. We're not too bad are we? Wait till we get him on to oxygen, you won't know him."

I was home in a flash. No rush hour, no gridlocks, no pile-ups. Gridlocks are new, I can remember thinking as my mind flopped about like a stranded fish. We are used to traffic jams here. There were none in Balclutha when I was a child. I can remember Dad's excitement years ago at the first set of traffic lights, on the corner of somewhere and somewhere, and what does it matter. There might be hundreds of them now. I'll never know, not unless I ask the family, or what's left. Just Ben and Doug with their iron-man faces and stubble-headed young and busy busy wives.

It was several years after we were married before Dad (fair haired, known as Snow) confided to me that he'd never got to grips with Olly, and he was sorry because obviously there was a lot there. Bit of a weirdo though wasn't he; wouldn't know a big end from his arse, excuse his French.

Mum said nothing.

I turned off the engine, realised I was shaking as I sat staring at the mess in the garage. Some people had tidy garages and sheds. Snow *stowed* his tools, hung them on nails in front of painted black cutouts of themselves. Spanners, screwdrivers, pliers, all had silhouettes, including the saws: pruning, tenon, fret, rip, all lined up. I spent a lot of time in the shed with Snow as a child, wiped down his cleaned tools with oily rags, brought him his smoko, swept the floor. He made me earrings from pale shells; we left riddles for each other on the workbench by the plane.

Q. *Why did the lobster blush?*
A. *Because it saw Queen Mary's bottom.*

I was not with him when he died.

A large spider with black iron pincers crept from its hiding place and slid across the invisible strands of its web to a halfmummified fly; one wing stuck upwards, the rest lay wrapped inside its body bag. Four of the spider's legs pointed ahead, the others backwards. The front ones embraced the fly, lined it up against its own head in a grotesque two-bodied form and continued spinning.

My mother also believed in good husbandry; she put eggs down in isinglass to see her through the winter, preserved fruit, and spun and knitted dark fleeces for work jerseys and white ones into shawls for babies.

36

They, the shawls, had to be fine enough to pull through a wedding ring. Even as a child I had wondered why; Snow didn't know either but we both knew it had to be.

The spider kept spinning. I felt sick. You don't have to watch it, you fool. Ring Copper. Now.

I sat by the telephone in the hall, jumped as the thing rang by my right haunch. "Hi, Mum. Check my e-mails would you, I'm expecting . . ."

My voice sounded hesitant, old. "It's Dad. He's in hospital."

"Christ. What?"

"A cardiac incident. Not serious apparently. We'll go and see him tonight."

"Hell yes. Don't worry about the e's. See you soon."

Copper put down the receiver, dragged one hand down his face. Olly in hossie. Bugger.

The timing was bad. Just when he had been working up to a serious talk with Dad. Such talks punctuated the past, memorable as the power poles stalking the Desert Road and about as useless, from the point of parental guidance.

You couldn't *talk* to him, that was the problem. He simply agreed with everything you said. Olly had listened to his complaints, had been concerned when he dropped Latin but said he realised it must be Copper's choice. Had agreed that most teachers were a bit of a trial, but they were underpaid, poor brutes, and it was an appalling business, teaching. Had he ever told Copper about his own teaching career?

And so it had gone on.

By all means Copper could leave college and form a pop group if he was convinced that was his vocation. Had Copper thought of a name? Olly would give it some thought.

Even his precipitate marriage did not seem to have upset his father unduly. He was sure Corinne (how did you spell it — two nn's or i-n-e? Ah the former was it, like the French) was a nice young woman when you got to know her. He liked her hair, he said, it reminded him of cornsilk, artificial of course and rather sticky but definitely reminiscent of those green-gold threads spilling from corn husks. Americans talk about shucking corn. Much nicer than boring old peeling, didn't Copper think.

Copper hadn't replied. He gave up temporarily, flung himself into Corinne's arms and wept, which surprised her until she decided tears meant passion and acted accordingly.

So why was he still trying to get through to the old man? Because he couldn't stop, that was why. Also, what would he do for money when he left WINZ.

He thought of last Thursday. Their usual half-baked conversation, his own pissy needling. It was always worse when they were alone, and Thursdays was Mum's night class in Upholstery or some such — she'd been going for years, God knows why.

"*Fate cannot touch me, I have dined tonight,*" Olly had said, pushing a slab of pallid underbelly of pastry to the edge of his plate. "Who said that, Copper?"

"I don't know, I never have. Why don't you look it up? After four thousand quotes, you owe the poor guy something."

"One of those things one should find out before shuffling off, you mean? Like brushing up on the stars, movements of planets, things of that nature?"

Copper clattered plates about and headed for the sink. It would have been better to let the conversation, if you could call it that, drop. It always was when Olly got on to eternals. But nit-picking at the old guy was a hard habit to break. "Because it doesn't make sense," he said. "Not in this case."

Olly shifted his buttocks and leaned forward. Abstracts, argument, logical or illogical discussions still stirred him. He put one hand over another and waited. "In what way?"

Copper tossed him a bone. "Because whoever said *Fate cannot touch me etc.* meant that the meal he had just finished had been so superb that nothing Fate or the gods could throw at him would matter."

"But that's the whole point," said Olly, bouncing about on the ill-padded bones of his behind. "The meal had been so celestial it was worth even death."

"That's the whole point, yes, but not tonight. A gourmet like you, Olly, can't say Grandma Gemmel's gluey Steak and Kidney Pie, oily hash browns and undercooked stir fry are worth risking the wrath of the gods for."

Olly had paused. "The blue was good."

"The blue was rampant, straining at the leash."

Last Thursday's stinking blue was symptomatic of both the Perkins' familial ties and his father's reaction to life. One of his childhood memories was of his mother shrinking back with one hand at her breast as Olly broached the half Stilton. He had bought it for an exorbitant price direct from the importer and treated it for months as though it were some sort of sacred archaeological site. Bore samples had been taken periodically, brandy inserted, damp cloths applied. Copper's reaction when he first saw Simone Martini's *Annunciation* in Florence on his OE had been a loud snorting laugh. The shrinking dismay of the reluctant Madonna to the Archangel's tidings had swung him straight to the cheese-broaching in Thorndon.

A dim little memory, as were so many. Childhood itself had seemed a bit dim to Copper. The Thorndon house had lead lattice windows and small rooms and not much talk. Not much was said at meal times and less when he had "gone off to play". He usually hung about from sheer boredom, watching the dining rituals of his father. The care and attention given to the pepper mill, for example. When it became empty Olly would unscrew it, remove the wooden lid and the little screw on the top and place them alongside as a subtle hint to Hester to refill it before the next meal.

Nobody used the pepper mill other than Olly, nor the complicated piece of glassware which ensured the oil and vinegar for his dressing remained inviolate till they hit his lettuce, whereupon they became vinaigrette, another culinary high point from thirty-five years ago to be ignored by Hester and mooned over by Olly as he tossed the green stuff about, ground his pepper and salt and banged on about his salad days when he was green in judgement. The more time-consuming the ritual, the further Hester retreated, the more fixed her gaze became on the good show of bronze chrysanthemums beyond the window.

Too much spoils the flavour, warned the label from the tin of Colman's mustard. Olly told Copper that although this seemed to be a kindly warning from the manufacturer it was a well-known fact that Mr Colman had made his fortune from the mustard left on the diner's plate. Better, he told his deadpan son and wife, to take small amounts at a time, two, possibly three. Someone must stand up to Mr Colman.

Offal of any kind, pig's trotters, brawn, sweetbreads, kidney, tripe and oxtail were his father's constant request.

So why did Mum do it? The thought had been with Copper for years. Hester was a strong character, more so than Olly, surely. So why did she deal with the offal she hated, take the pepper mill hint, cherish the pompous old pot's every wish.

The only time Copper remembered Olly taking a moral stand had shaken them all. In 1981 he had announced, sitting at the end of the table and bonging his face with a napkin, that he would be joining the anti-apartheid protest marchers in their attempt to stop the Springboks versus All Blacks match at Athletic Park the following Saturday. He understood that one of the rallying points was to be near the National Museum. Would Copper give him the exact time and place?

Copper continued sucking an oxtail vertebra in the otherwise stunned silence, then licked his fingers and summed up: "But you don't care about apartheid, Dad."

"Don't you think it's about time you stopped sucking your bones."

"But you don't. You don't care about anything."

Olly straightened his shoulders. "I care very deeply about injustice. Apartheid," he said, "is legalised racism condoned by law."

"Yeah, I read that too. I suppose it's because they're so far away, the victims, I mean."

"That's enough, Copper," said Hester. She turned to Oliver: "That's good news, Olly, I'm meeting the Brownstones. I've got all the details."

The large crowd milled about, stamped their feet, greeted each other. "Look, there's Ron," said Hester, "and Nan. And the Hodleys, all that way."

The heterogeneous crowd was exhilarated, some eager, some earnest, some angry and more hostile since the recent batoning in Molesworth Street. Some seemed faintly pleased with themselves and their solidarity. "Fancy the Hodleys," murmured Hester again.

The crowd grew larger as they listened silent and attentive to a tough-looking Marshal with a loud hailer, an armband, a motorbike helmet and a wooden shield. They were to link arms, hold tight, keep in step, stay near a Marshal at all times. If they could. Squads were marching from all over Wellington, he bellowed.

Eventually they would all converge on Rintoul Street, join forces at Athletic Park, break through the barricades, stop the bloody Test, then head off for a beer. Right? And finally, if things got rough, keep your heads down and stay calm. The crowd roared approval.

"I've never seen you not calm," whispered Hester to Olly as Copper disappeared to find his mates.

Olly adjusted his cap, murmured a nervous "May I?" and took the arm of the gaunt woman beside him.

Hester clutched the other. "I do love you," she said, squeezing his arm.

They set off. He looked down at her, smiling. "I feel like an extra at the battle of Peterloo."

"Who?"

"Tell you later."

Led by the chanting Marshals in their makeshift gear, the squad swung up Taranaki Street. The chants grew louder and more aggressive as they marched up Wallace Street. Citizens who would hesitate to appropriate a Disabled carpark were shouting:

> One, two, fuck the cops,
> Three, four, fuck the cops,
> And more, fuck the cops
> One, two, fuck the . . .

Tension mounted; they were united against racial discrimination seven thousand miles away. They were doing something, they were marching in protest. They were in earnest.

One, two, and again, roared Hester with the crowd.

After some time Oliver slowed, dragged his feet, had to be chivvied along. "I don't want to fuck the cops," he yelled as they marched past the Old Show Buildings.

Hester turned to him, "What?"

"The cops, I don't want to . . ."

"Oh Lord." She unlinked arms with John Brownstone, pulled Olly to the side of the road. "You don't want *what?*"

"To fuck the cops."

"Dear God. What are you on about now?"

The marchers were still passing, heading down the slope towards Adelaide Road.

"That chant. I have no wish to fuck the cops. I have every respect for the New Zealand Police Force or had until recently. It's Muldoon and the thick-headed oafs at the Rugby Union who should be impregnated."

"There's no requirement for you to *do* anyone. It's a *chant*."

"I never say, let alone chant, anything I don't mean. I'm leaving."

"No!" she said in fury. "I know what you're doing. You're a coward, that's all, a pathetic coward and trying to make a virtue of it."

Olly looked at her in blinking astonishment. "If you think that, there's not much point in continuing the conversation."

"No, no, there isn't." She turned and ran down the slope after the stragglers, stopped and swung around. "You can finish your crossword," she cried and blundered on.

"Wait," he said, and threw her the car keys.

44

She came home from Rintoul Street late in the afternoon in a state of shock, with a weeping graze on her right cheek. She refused to talk about it. She refused to talk about anything. It was horrible, horrible.

Oliver, appalled, took her in his arms and put her to bed, crooned comfort and dressed her cheek with iodine which stung.

"I'll never vote National again. Never," she said.

"I haven't since the Bastion Point debacle."

"Why didn't you tell me?"

"I didn't think you'd be interested."

"I'm your *wife*."

"And Snow Hope's daughter. What a defection. It would have killed him."

She stared past his shoulder with wide eyes. "The police, the fight at Rintoul Street. I can't tell you what it was like. I was terrified, we all were. When they come at you with those long batons." She shuddered.

"I should have been there to look after you."

She made an odd sound, something between a gasp and a sniff. "It's not *that*."

He kissed her forehead. "I'll boil you an egg," he said.

She was asleep when he went in to remove the untouched tray. Later when he crept into bed beside her she rolled over.

"I know you're not a coward."

"Good."

"I just had to say something."

"Of course you did. Don't worry about it. I'm not very good at discussing things."

45

Her hand touched him. "Nnnn," she said.

Copper did not appear till next morning. He had lost a front tooth.

CHAPTER
FOUR

I was awake when they arrived and glad to see them, very glad. I offered my cheek to Hester, shook hands with Copper. Smiling inanely, like a nervous hostess apologising for inadequacies no one else had thought of, I explained that unfortunately I wouldn't be in a single room for long.

"There's a new chap breathing down my neck, you see. There are only two single rooms, both near the nurses' station, that's what they call it, *station*, so the staff can keep an eye on the newest cot cases. You don't last long in a single, I gather, not unless you're in extremis."

I shook Copper's hand again. "Copper," I said, "nice to see you."

"God, Dad, you look a mess."

"God had nothing to do with it, or I hope not. Stop giving me the breeze up."

"But you do. Terrible, man."

"Too kind."

"Nonsense," said Hester. "You look wonderful, miles better."

"Yes, and wait for the good news," I said. "There was no coronary apparently. Just what they call a 'cerebral incident'. Nice phrase, don't you think, for a bit of a wobbly? Could happen to anyone. I'll be out in a few days, then I come back later for some other 'procedure', they call it. An echocardiogram. I'm not to go back to work till after that, unfortunately. About a fortnight they say."

Naked and vulnerable as a beached whale I lay supine on the couch in the Echocardiogram Unit, awaiting assistance. The whale, however, would be prone, its palms-down flippers making ineffectual movements in the sand in its attempt at take-off. Its companions have sailed with the tide. He/she has missed the bus.

Whale rescues are a feature of southern summers. Volunteers work day and night to help the stranded. They are filmed and shown on television as a feel-good item at the close of the six o'clock News programme just before the weather. First the helpers must keep the whale alive by pouring sea water over it until the next high tide. People run to and fro with buckets; wet sacks come into play. The flotation techniques vary but they all involve physical effort on the part of the rescuers, a demonstration of enthusiastic volunteers at work.

Best of all is when the cameras catch the mammal as it takes off for the open sea, and men, women and children shout and throw bright hats in the air as they wave Godspeed. After which a large tanned man with a sunburned nose will tell the camera that with any luck the ex-stranded will rejoin the pod.

If the rescue does not succeed the coverage tends to be shorter and is not the last news item that evening. A different spokesman, equally tanned but unsmiling, tells the viewers that the team is gutted.

I have never felt so ridiculously stark naked, so totally in the buff. Patting a hand about in search of cover, I found a small green square of cloth beneath my left buttock, pulled it out and laid it over the wrinkled privates.

Bored, chilly and not at my best I was halfway through a yawn when the door swung open and a cardiac technician bustled in with that quick swish of white-robed authority found in hospitals. On her left breast a brooch in the shape of a pink ceramic parrot announced *Hi, I'm Denise*.

Its owner gave a genteel yelp. "Ooh, you didn't need to take off *everything*. Just to the waist, I said."

"Oh."

"It doesn't worry me," said Denise, "I just thought . . ."

"Never mind. I'll remember next time."

Denise doubled with mirth. "You'll be lucky, what with them all queuing up for this guy." Banging large pillows about, she indicated the machine blinking to itself in the corner. "Meet Eddie Echo," she said.

I gave the thing a curt nod. Denise's car would have a pet name too. There are some things you can put money on.

"I'll get you into the correct position," she said and continued her slapping, this time of me. "Heave up, lean forward, back a bit, now maintain. *Maintain*. The angle is all important. There. Right. Hold. Watch if you want to," she said kindly. "Most of them do."

I aimed my pale chest at the screen and held.

The pumping, squelching movement of the heart was interesting to watch in a meaty uncooked sort of way.

"Look at the valves," said Denise, pointing. "Sweet, aren't they."

I agreed. Definitely the best part, those small fluttering wings of tissue endlessly raising and lowering to open and to close. So strong and yet so delicate, there was nothing robotic or mechanical about them. They were frilly, fragile-looking things, strangely eerie in appearance.

The effort involved in the whole process was also impressive. All that previously hidden thumping and squeezing and fluttering, to say nothing of the sounds of liquid sloshing about. Fundamental plumbing sounds too, no sacred vessels here. A workman-like affair, the heart, with you all the way to the end.

Denise clicked a switch on the machine; a blue line jiggled and was still. "Just pop your clothes on. I'll see you next door in a minute."

I put on my clothes with relief. I could get out now. Clothed, I could made a break for it. Instead I picked up a battered magazine from the table and read, *This classic Russian conibiac is an elaborate dish of salmon layered with crepes and a rich sauce. It may be . . .*

Denise crashed in waving the echocardiogram result in the air. "Wow," she cried, "you've got a lovely heart."

"Oh . . ."

She clapped her hands together. "I bet you've taken good care of it. It's amazing for a man of your age."

"I walk to the surgery and back every day," I lied. Not every day but I wanted to get away from this mad woman and her daft parrot.

"Nothing better. Nothing. I wish I had the discipline."

Discipline, I thought. I, Oliver Perkins, have discipline and a lovely heart.

To own a heart which has not been overworked, which has been cared for as though it were a vintage car, is surely a good thing. Yet I felt a perverse sense of annoyance, not pride, as though I had deliberately kept an early Meccano engine in mint condition, no pieces missing and its box unmarked. A collector's item, not something which had been well played with, tossed about or loved to death, which seemed the more laudable fate for toys.

It is idiotic, I know, to conflate praise for the genuine article, that efficient, hard-working internal pump, with some seventeenth-century poet's conceit about the storehouse of emotions, the source of love and the seat of anguish. Nevertheless, thoughts of hearts tumbled about me: passionate hearts, valiant, broken, wild or bleeding, hearts singing or heavy as lead, as good as gold or mean as muckworms — all, all had been *used*. And these millions of hearts had had trillions of words written about them and I couldn't remember any of them other than the singing bird which I have always found rather an attractive image.

My mind was a blank; I could remember nothing. I was irritated, edgy, and would remain so until I could look up Hearts in the *Oxford Dictionary of Quotations*.

More depressing still was the knowledge that the cared-for, the virtually pristine heart, a heart unbroken, unbleeding and certainly unwild, was unlikely to feature in any line of poetry worth finding.

Denise's comments had given me food for thought, even though I knew I was being ridiculous. A clean bill of heart for a septuagenarian is excellent news, an achievement to admit to when chatting with non-existent mates over a mythical beer.

"Thank you," I said. "That's good news."

"Now just pop along to the cardiologist in the main waiting room."

"Thank you," I said again.

Pop. During my days in the ward last month I had been invited to pop in every conceivable direction: out, over, down, left, right or centre. Pop was the one-stop verb for carers.

Dr Martin the cardiologist was an amiable man, well dressed, friendly, a good-humoured dynamo around the ward. I had murmured doggerel in praise of him in the blue-lit nights in the ward.

I've a nifty little pocket on my backside,
With a little tab and button just for that side,
And I'm seen about the ward doing good wher'er
*   I'm called,*
With that nifty little pocket on my backside.

"Excellent, just what I expected of course," he said, "but the dizziness had to be checked. I think we can forget the whole incident now, don't you agree?"

52

"Yes, thank you."

We shook hands.

Hester was waiting in the Corolla. She is good at waiting.

"Hullo," she said. "What did he say?"

"He says the incident is closed. No further bulletins will be issued."

She patted my knee. "Excellent!"

There is something proprietorial about knee-patting. I moved my leg slightly, tugged the safety belt with force.

The car lurched backwards, brakes slammed, forward impetus was achieved.

"*Hippety hoppity, here comes the wapiti,*" I murmured.

"Your driving is a great deal worse than mine," she said, sailing past a large four-wheel drive labelled *Bighorn* on its alarmingly sized spare wheel.

"True. But I'm ten years older. I could have lurched my way home somehow."

"We didn't know that when we came."

I looked in the rear-vision mirror. "Why are those thugs of things always driven by long-legged blondes."

"What else did they say?"

"That I have a lovely heart and must have taken good care of it."

Blind corner. Tricky bit. Silence.

"Say it again," she said eventually.

"I have a lovely heart and must have taken good care of it."

"Oh," said Hester.

Ah, the joys of being back in harness, of business as usual; the sight of the blue Planmeca Prostyle, of Miss de Lillo's face glowing with welcome, her hands clasped as if to contain her rapture.

But best of all, I think, is the comfort of routine. Of Nato Standards and "Rinse please", of amalgams and partial plates.

Mrs Stubbs was there the first day I came back, poor woman. God knows why she didn't seek alternative oral assistance while I was away but I felt it was not my place to enquire.

The joys of home I had already visited. The reassurance of putting out a tentative foot at three in the morning and discovering carpet rather than the foreign chill of hospital vinyl; of finding Hester silent beside me rather than being surrounded by the goitrous hawks and explosive snores of sedated men. The strong male crescendo rising to its thundering climax could be dramatic in itself, but it was by no means soporific.

The dim light of the ward may also have contributed to my sleepless nights, *nuits blanches* as the French call them. Whatever the cause, I did a lot of conceptual work (a Copper phrase) in Ward Eleven. A bad time and a bad place for it, one might think; nevertheless I thought long and hard during my nights in the coronary ward.

So much so that one part of my daily routine which has not survived the trauma of my cardiac incident is the maintenance of my journal. It had seemed important when I began it, but no longer. I have found I prefer thinking, which also takes up a lot of time — time spent not necessarily pleasantly but in an interesting and worthwhile way. I did make occasional notes. I suppose they could be described as thoughts. *Perkins' pensées* perhaps. A cardiac incident, be it mild, certainly concentrates the mind.

Here I am, I remember thinking as the clang of an urgent urinal met a steel pole nearby, a healthy man of seventy-five. I have enough money, a modest competence, as Charles Octavius used to say. I have food, warmth, shelter. I have never been, and I hope never to be, shot at. I have a charming wife who is ten years younger, always a good idea if one is in for the long haul, and one reasonably pleasant adult offspring, or as reasonably pleasant as any haphazard selection of parental genes is liable to be. And then there is Poppy. My Poppy Esther.

So, Perkins, I thought during the snorting, snore-ridden nights, you are a very lucky man.

This tempting of fate did not worry me. I have always been pragmatic about my good fortune, none of that guilt-ridden middle-class angst for me. No, the thing which disturbed me most came later, with Denise's enthusiasm for the pristine condition of my heart.

Which brings me to something I must confide even if it is only to myself. I don't consider myself heartless or

55

uncaring of the interests of others. In fact there are one or two who might vouch for my good-heartedness — Miss de Lillo perhaps, or Mrs Stubbs. Their Get Well cards this time were positively effusive. No rabbits, no stethoscopes. Just roses, roses all the way, full grown and blowsy, though Mrs Stubbs' offering had a few pink buds. But then Miss de Lillo and Mrs Stubbs are, how shall I say, peripheral as regards my emotions. Pleasant women both, but nothing to do with the workings at my heart's core. There is no reason why they should be; I imagine they would both run like riggers if I intimated anything to the contrary.

But Hester. What about Hester, my true wife Hester. It is an extraordinary admission to have to make, but I feel I have not, perhaps, taken enough interest in Hester's happiness over the last forty years. Oh, we have made love ten thousand times with mutual pleasure, we have rolled and sweated and rocked about in the best two-hander in the business. We have laughed, we have made up, in fact I don't remember many occasions when the necessity to do so — make up, I mean — has arisen.

We understand each other, Hester and I; we have moulded together, become accommodated to each other as a soft shoe accommodates to a bunion. Ah, but there's the . . . No, I refuse to say "rub". But I feel I have not put my heart into the non-bed side of affection. As I see things now, Hester has been the pliant soft-leathered one. She has been the accommodater, I the accommodee. The bunion if you like.

56

Which is all right. Quite all right. Except that it seems a little unfair. Should I perhaps take more interest in her pursuits? But what does she pursue? Hobbies, for example? Upholstery perhaps? Surely not. No one could expect one's spouse to be interested in upholstery unless they shared the passion to refurbish. To most of us the intricacies of upholstery are as esoteric as those of early Byzantine coinage. I can't think why she still goes to classes each Thursday when practically every chair, sofa or stool in the house is stuffed to the gunwales already.

So what other pursuits does she have? She gardens with fervour and reads with verve, she does good things, she helps, she gives, she has friends. She learns the Maori language, plays club croquet, is an expert on Danish cross-stitch. We are knee deep in cross-stitch bell-pulls, we have clothes embroidered with merry folk dancing with reindeer.

We both enjoy films. Why then do we so seldom go together? Inertia on my part? Possibly. But also she is knowledgeable about them, has favourite directors, knows their previous works, that sort of thing. Which is beyond me. I just like going to the flicks. Miss Stratton and I never discussed camera angles. If the good guy beat the bad guy we were happy and if the custard pies flew we were happier.

I do see, almost, why Hester prefers to go to films with or without her fellow aficionados, Jan or Heather or her best friend Joyce Polt. Besides she usually goes to matinees, so that lets me out of that one.

What do other men do to show they care for their wives? Take them out for a meal perhaps. But where? And indeed why, when the food is so much better at home. Similarly the flowers she grows are better than those I could buy for her from Blossoms Galore. Also I am the wrong generation and nationality for that gesture. Mature antipodean men are scared of florists and their flowers. Apart from the cost, their offerings are liable to die on you, to wilt or implode within hours. They have no staying power, these overbred tokens of esteem.

As for asking people to share our excellent meals. The problem here is that the rituals of hospitality are based on a system of revenge. They might ask us back.

I remember the last time we took the initiative in entertaining friends — that is Hester's friends Joyce Polt and Heather Coley and their respective husbands, Claude and Douglas. I made them welcome, or so I thought, I listened to Claude (money market) and Douglas (options), I poured wine, I smiled and smiled and smiled again.

They left, we did the dishes, me with the towel, Hester at the sink in an apron with spoonbills and her hair shining beneath the light. Have I mentioned that her hair is still dark? Unusual, I understand, for women of her age though by no means unattractive. Be that as it may, she turned to me with a dripping wine glass in a yellow-gloved hand and said with passion, and I use the word advisedly, "I'm never going to do that again."

"Oh, I thought it went quite well. Very well," I said quickly.

"You hated it, didn't you?"

"Me? No, not at all."

"I saw you looking at your watch."

"Surely not. I was most careful to keep my wrist under the table."

She swung around, now clutching a scrubber. "No. That's it. No more. Never, never again. You hate it, and I can see my friends elsewhere. All my friends, each and every one. It's hopeless. I know you try. You can't help it, but no, no, no. Never again."

I should have tried harder, I should have dissembled, I see that now. Even with that ghaster Polt. After all, it required little effort to keep him happy other than to nod occasionally with wonder at his achievements and the amount of money he was making and, admittedly more difficult, to laugh at his grisly jokes.

Hester and I made love later. Rather memorable it was too, I seem to remember. Perhaps it was gratitude on my part. We shall never know.

Yes, I must undoubtedly do something to demonstrate my love and enthusiasm for her. Not to attempt the possession of a well-used heart, dear God no, nor because of my glimpse at the thump and slurps of its workings. However, Denise's excitement has undoubtedly made me think.

And what if Hester died first? The thought is, no . . . it cannot be thought.

Miss de Lillo has brought me my Nato Standard. Routine glides on. I am greatly blessed as Mrs Stratton, my first corpse, used to say, but I must do something to gladden my wife's heart.

Suggestions for ways to achieve this:

I must "give more" of myself. How?

I must "keep my friendships in repair". How?

I must "reach out". No, don't let's put it like that. Outreach is one of Copper's more alarming words.

Fill full my heart, that I may go forth . . . No, no, no, not that either.

Only one more patient this morning. Upper Left Canine, Mr Bettoli from along the road.

CHAPTER
FIVE

I met Hester at the front gate on my return from the day's work. Quite a pretty scene it was: she was reaching for a high branch of a climbing rose, a torn nylon stocking clenched between her teeth. She was unable to speak, of course, but demonstrated by vigorous nodding of head and rolling of eyes that I should remove the stocking.

"Thhhh," she said, bending the branch down for me to tie in place.

She was flushed and attractive, or as attractive as a sixty-five-year-old woman in Strength-through-Joy tramping boots is likely to be. "I'm going for a walk up the hill," she said.

"Wait till I change and I'll come too."

Her nose wrinkled, an odd gesture, not indicative of pleasure. "Why?"

"I thought it might be nice."

"Why?"

"Husbands and wives do occasionally go for walks together."

"When in the last forty years have you suggested my going for a walk with you? You walk faster than me. My pace is all wrong, remember. You can't have forgotten."

I tried again. "I just thought it might be nice."

"You've left it a bit late," she laughed and strode off, swinging her way toward the dark pines of Tinakori Hill. "Very Caspar Friedrich, those pines," Copper tells me in Art Speak. "They have strong verticality."

They go upwards.

I went inside, took off my jacket and treated myself to an untouched crossword from my diminishing store. I felt faintly rejected — well no, rejected is too strong; deflated might be better.

I remembered the days we had walked together up and down and over and around Dunedin from Flagstaff to Signal Hill, from Mount Cargill to the blue penguins nesting beyond Portobello. She must have become slower, I suppose.

One day I'll never forget, on our way up to the albatrosses' breeding ground at the tip of the peninsula. I can see the track of flattened grass wide enough for two, sense the crisp new air blowing from Antarctica and the feel of her tough little hand in mine as we laughed together, and me thinking, This is Love, this is what they mean by it. To be alive and delight in being so, every breath a miracle.

We were a bit late in the season for the albatrosses, most of them had left, but there were a few fed-up-looking parents with their tail-end-Charlie offspring squatting alongside. Half fluff, half feather, as clumsy and awkward as any other teenager.

"Let's get married," I said and bent to kiss her throat where the pulse beats. Her beret fell as her head

62

tipped back. It lay there, a golden disc on the windswept grass.

"Yes," she said. "Now."

I tried to concentrate on my *Times* crossword. I had cracked six across, a tough clue the conquest of which would normally have kept me happy for hours. Question (5 letters). *Jones takes the plunge*. Answer. *Inigo*.

It is in such moments that I most miss my other friend, Godfrey Tollance, also dead regrettably. A skilled crossword man and always receptive to my boastful calls. He was also a generous sharer. More generous than me. I would have yielded Inigo, but not without a certain amount of nudging. But tonight even Inigo did not give me that sweet nip of intellectual smugness. No, my thoughts were of Hester striding up the hill. The scorn on her face had reminded me of the anti-Springbok Tour march and her cry, "Go home to your crossword."

She apologised certainly, but the memory rankles. I sensed then that my crosswords had become, for her, something of an alien presence in the house. An incubus perhaps, like a dog which is devotedly loyal to your spouse and treats you with jowl-curling contempt.

When we were first married we did the puzzles together, but then in those days we did everything together including washing each other's hair in the bath, which seems rather odd now. But crosswords, for her, have palled. She is not a lateral thinker, Hester, though her general knowledge is good along the lines of "Name of Napoleon's horse".

Enough of crosswords. I was on edge, waiting tense and eager for Hester to come home. To take off those goshawful shoes and come and sit on my knee and talk to me, or rather to listen to me while I revealed my plan to delight her. A plan so breathtakingly simple I was stunned that it had never occurred to me before. But then, of course, the necessity to delight Hester had not occurred to me until sparked off by those two wise fools. Denise and her pink parrot were locked in my mind like a double act, the galah being the fall-guy to Denise's cryptic wisdom.

The front door opened. I leapt up and more or less ran to fling it wide. Hester was pinker than ever (quite a steep pull up that hill) and more than cheerful. I tried to take her in my arms but she laughed, pulled off her parka and tossed it to me while she dealt with the clodhoppers.

"Come and sit on my knee," I said, "I've had the most wonderful idea."

Still tugging at the boots she looked up me, her expression indicating both astonishment and hilarity. "On your knee?"

"Well, not if you don't want to. I just thought it might be nice."

"That's what you said before."

"No, I didn't."

"Not sitting on knees, nutter. Going for walks with me. You said it would be nice."

"So it would have been, I can't understand why . . ."

She leaned against the wall looking puzzled, genuinely puzzled, I could see that. "Olly, what's going on?"

I straightened a reproduction Picasso print of a small satyr playing a flute behind her left shoulder and took her hand. "Come and I'll tell you. I'll get us a glass of wine."

"Olly, it's Thursday. And Copper wants a serious talk with you." She kissed my left ear. "Tell me later," she said and ran up the stairs. She moves quickly Hester — darts about, here, there, gone in a moment.

Damn. Thursday. Bloody Thursday. The first incomprehensible joke I remember concerned Thursdays. A cartoon of one hippopotamus up to its nostrils in mud was saying to another, *I keep thinking it's Thursday*. I asked Charles Octavius to explain. He looked up from the copy of *Punch* which was destined for what he rather grandly called "my chambers". "The joke is," he said after some time, "that hippopotamuses don't have Thursdays."

This seemed to me at the time understandable but not very funny. Which is pretty much how I have felt about Thursdays ever since Hester began taking night classes in Upholstery for Beginners a thousand years ago.

And not only a Thursday but also a talk, undoubtedly a serious one, with Copper. Tonight of all nights. Double damn.

At my instigation he bought fried oysters rather than dogfish. Oysters were two shillings and sixpence a dozen when his mother and I were in Dunedin, but I refrained from mentioning the fact. Like all young, or youngish, Copper is quick to decry repetition and one mustn't be a bore. My dead friend Godfrey Tollance told me once that his son had called him a bloody old bore. I was surprised, but Godfrey said it could have been a lot worse and I suppose there is something in that. I did wonder for a moment what would have been my father's reaction if I had offered him the same comment, but there are some things which are beyond even the most fertile of imaginations.

The oysters were excellent, the chips not bad. The blue vein, however, was again on its way out. I waded through my piece but Copper declined with a pained sniff. Silence continued. If Copper wanted a serious talk, he could lead from his corner.

Which eventually he did. "Dad," he said.

"Yes," I said, helping myself to another malodorous hunk in a small gesture of defiance, antagonism, God knows what.

"I'd like to have a talk with you."

Oh, Gawd. Diversion, delay, anything was worth trying. "Shall we sit in the soft chairs next door?" I said.

"They're not soft," he said. "Your behind bounces about like a bloody yo-yo."

"Yes, she does tend to overdo the stuffing."

Clutching our coffee mugs we padded through. I aimed for the softest chair but Copper beat me by a short head. He is heavy in the bottom, my son, and treats it with respect. He put his mug down with a deep sigh: "I can't stand WINZ another minute."

I put my mug down with equal care. "Ah."

"I'm going to quit."

"Are you?"

"Is that all you have to say?"

I straightened my shoulders. Effort, attention was the thing. I said something to the effect that it must be very difficult to work in a government department where funding is at a premium and . . .

He was unimpressed. "Name me one that isn't."

"I hadn't finished," I said. "All government departments say they are short of cash but . . ." His mouth opened but I swept on ". . . but I imagine it must be far more stressful for the staff where they are dealing directly with human miseries, the concerns and worries of clients face to face."

That thrusting jaw, that floating hair. "What do you know about human misery?"

"Very little, but I imagine the day-to-day relations between the state and its poorest citizens must be trying on both sides."

"*Trying,*" snorted Copper. "You've got no idea, none at all. It's the frustration, the grinding never-ending frustration. You try and do your job, you know there's never enough money. And not only money. Not enough time. Not enough patience. The clients hate you. Who wouldn't? I feel I'm bled dry, dry as a kosher lamb."

"Is that what they call compassion fatigue?" I said after a pause.

He gave me a look of undiluted contempt. And hatred too, or something too near it for comfort.

"I try and tell you what it's like, how I can't go on, how I've had it up to here. I'm whacked, rigid, useless, and all you do is check you've got the right phrase, the correct words. Forget the words!" He flung himself forward, hid his unruly hair in his hands.

The seat of the chair bounced slightly.

I was moved, definitely moved. He had been such a funny little boy; curly auburn hair, gentle, his hands soft then, not bony like his mother's. Kind to beetles, small animals. A serious little bloke, our Copper. Now his shoulders were moving. Surely he was not weeping. I gave a slight cough.

He lifted his head, wiped the back of his hand too near his nose and stared at me. The tears in his eyes had reddened the corneas, deepened the irises to bright stinging blue.

"Sorry," he sniffed, whether in apology for the tears or the nose or the general hell of everything, I had no way of knowing.

Maybe it was the fierceness of the blazing blue eyes or possibly the unyielding seat of my chair but I was becoming increasingly uncomfortable. I put out an apologetic hand. "Sorry, that was an unhelpful remark."

He didn't take the hand, but smiled. He has a good smile, Copper, warm and friendly, if infrequent. "Forget it," he said and stared at his boots. "WINZ," he sighed. "It's all there, in the acronym. Can't you hear the cheers in the executive washroom when some high-priced idiot came up with it. Positive, snappy and of course visionary, as visionary as blowing $79,000 for the design alone of the corporate wardrobe. Whatever happened to the public service ethic, accountability?" He leaned back, a man seeking answers I was unable to give. "The place is hell for staff, let alone clients."

I refrained from commenting on the words "corporate wardrobe" but the phrase has always interested me. I assume it originated in the United States, as did "executive washroom".

But there is the puzzle. If the American closet has the same meaning as the English wardrobe, should not the phrase be the "corporate closet"? The expression "to come out of the closet" has a resonance about it, definitely more grunt. "To come out of the wardrobe" merely sounds ludicrous — what would the man or woman be doing there in the first place? Whereas the word closet positively reeks of privacy.

I hadn't meant to digress from Copper's problems. I apologised to him in silence.

I felt, not for the first time, that there might have been ways in which I had failed my son, though in all conscience I can't think how. There is a phrase used by paediatricians and psychiatrists when discussing the role of the mother in the physical and mental development of her child. *A Good Enough Mother*. Apparently a perfect mother is hard to find. In fact a perfect mother, so Hester told me with glee, can wreck her offspring's life simply by being too perfect. I forget how exactly, but one obvious difficulty which might arise would be when the perfectly mothered, or fathered, offspring sets out to find the perfect mate. Especially, perhaps, the perfect wife.

To my mind Hester has always been much more than a good enough mother. She and Copper have always been close — not a word I like much, perhaps because my mother used it to describe badly aired rooms. Be that as it may, to me there is something faintly cloying about the expression. Not that you could describe Hester's and Copper's friendship in those terms. They like each other, they have silly jokes, they laugh. They sit in the same room for hours in silence, reading, writing, whatever, and one knows they are at ease with each other. Hester and I also enjoy our elected silences, but I am not so sure about Copper and me.

Perhaps closeness begins with ease, but damn it all, we can't all be close even if we would like to be. Obviously there must be such a thing as a Good Enough Father.

I pride myself on never having criticised Copland. I have left him to make his own decisions. Even his choice of Corinne as a wife, alarming as it was, seemed to me to be his own business. Hester, I know, found the fact more difficult to accept.

I had always been conscious of my own father's looming presence in my life. Charles Octavius's calm omniscience, his sure and certain knowledge that he had not only the right answer but also the best advice with which he was more than generous. Also there was his considerable erudition, not just in things classical, theological and legal but in everything beneath the sun. He told me once, I remember, that all Portuguese Generals are fat. I saw no reason to query the statement at the time. My astonishment now lies in the fact that I never did so.

I have no intention of mentioning these feelings about my father to Copper. I have never been a member of the Blame-it-on-the-Mum-and-Dad school of modern thought. In many cases of parenting this may be true, but not, I feel, for the offspring of Good Enough Parents.

Who was the hero who, when skewered by the tricky question from his wayward son, "Why did you have me then?", replied that if he had known how the son was going to turn out he would not have done so. Genes, yes: to ignore genetic inheritance is like putting a turkey in an oven and expecting scones. But how the Good Enough Parents' offspring turn out is dependent on many factors, some of them unknowable. *Is you is or is you ain't my baby* is not the whole answer.

I do remember being disappointed when Copper dropped Latin but in retrospect I don't give a damn. It was his choice. Life goes on. We are still in the ring. I do wonder, however, whether my laissez-faire attitude, my letting Copper find his own way, make his own decisions, might not have been as a result of Charles Octavius's, shall we say, blanket approach to my childhood. My father's fault after all, even unto the second generation. What a bit of luck.

An alternative thought, an unwelcome one (shades of Denise): might I never have *cared* enough about the concerns of my son, had declined to open my heart to him, not *guided* him. Had not, in fact, damn well loved him enough.

I throttled the thought. Self-indulgent wallowing has never appealed to me.

However, I must try harder to think of some words of comfort for my unhappy sack-like son.

To my amazement they came. "You must not blame yourself," I said. "Your grandfather, who sadly you never knew, had the same problem at one point in his career."

Copper looked at me with a tolerant but distant smile, one reminiscent of a bystander watching an incompetent busker flinging balls about.

"Let's have a whisky," he said.

"Whisky?"

He was on his feet, heading for the appropriate cupboard. He turned, smiled again. "We always have a whisky when we get on to Grandfather."

"Oh. Well, thank you. Just a small one."

He ignored my request as to size as any sensible man would do, and handed me the glass. There is something pleasing about an unexpected whisky, particularly from one's son. It wasn't his to give of course, but that is not the point. It was a gesture of goodwill for which I was grateful. We lifted our glasses to each other. Nodded.

"Tell me," he said, "which particular problem of Grandfather's was this one? He had a few, didn't he? Rather an itinerant sort of life."

I was annoyed and said so. "All those years in Cornwallis could never be described as itinerant."

"True," he said, "true. Wrong word. Try varied."

I nodded and told him the story of Charles Octavius's painful realisation that he must give up his vocation as a priest. I had filled in the background and was getting to the denouement and Charles's sense of failure when I realised that perhaps this might not be the comforting story I had intended.

I was right. Copper was on his feet, whisky splashing dangerously, his face a yard from mine. "I know that, I've heard it a thousand times and it makes me toss. Of all the egotistical, pretentious crap. We're meant to feel sorry for the old guy, not a thought for those he's dumped."

He took a large gulp of his whisky and moved even closer. I have always been alarmed by face-to-face proximity; I also dislike this ubiquitous and inaccurate use of the word crap. I edged back as he raged on.

"Why do you think I went into social work?"

I opened my mouth to say that I had sometimes wondered myself, but Copper was at full flood.

"I'll tell you why. Now listen . . . I went into social work because all I could see in the male Perkins line was years and years of self-interested, reactionary old buggers without an ounce of altruism among them."

I was on my feet. "That's enough. I will not listen to your fulminations against your forebears for another . . ."

"'Fulminations against your forebears.' You should be living in the Home Counties or the High Reaches or some other hole. You're a New Zealander!"

"Yes," I said.

I sat down, took a cautious sip. The silence continued. Copper sat scowling into his whisky. Scowling and whisky do not go together. A waste of both.

Some sort of apology seemed to be expected, though I couldn't understand why. WINZ might be an unpleasant place in which to work but comparisons with the conditions of those attempting to help the poor of the London slums of the 1890s were risible. Also wasn't *he*, Copper, about to "dump" his clients.

"I'm sorry," I said, "but I don't understand what you're talking about."

"Why don't you behave like someone in this part of the world. Become more involved. Here. The Pacific Rim. Where it's happening. Stop being so bloody Eurocentric."

Again I opened my mouth but he rolled on, a tsunami of hectoring aggression worthy of an investigative TV interviewer drowning the last squeaks of a scuppered MP.

I was, apparently, a phoney post-colonial reject with my copies of the *Independent on Sundays* and my *Times* crosswords, but worse than that I was stifling his mother's interest in her own country. Had I thought of that! I was attempting to live in some sort of a British enclave. A little England beyond the seas. A never-never land.

I put up my hand. Useless. Tried again, finally pulled out a white handkerchief and waved it in surrender. "Balls," I shouted. "Why shouldn't I?"

"Stifle Mum?"

"Don't be ridiculous. Why shouldn't I live as I please? Your views on my negative influence on your mother are ludicrous. She worships every inch of the country, loves the original people, always has. Slept on the marae recently, you remember. She and Joyce went on a bus, very interesting it was too except for her sore back."

"Typical! Everything's got to be a joke, making fools of everyone."

"I am *not making* . . ."

"Her sore back."

"What about it?"

"All you've got to say about Mum's interest in Maoritanga is she got a sore back sleeping at the marae."

I had him tooth and jowl. "No," I said, "it was the day before, digging in the garden, that wrecked her back."

He did me proud, my son. He fell back on his chair, flung his hands to his head and laughed. Laughed till the tears ran down his face and he could laugh no more. Finally he dragged a doubtful-looking bit of cloth from his pocket and banged it about his face. "Let's have another a whisky," he sobbed.

"Yes," I said, seizing the moment when we seemed to have reached calmer waters for my important question. "There's one point I must make. What do you intend to do when you leave WINZ?"

"Ah, yes." Copper leaned back, inspected the amber depths of his second whisky and gave me a shy glance. "I thought I might go back to Uni."

"At your age?"

"Why not?"

Why not indeed? And who pays, I thought, my pristine paint-fresh heart plummeting to my boots, and it does too, one can feel it. I saw the filmy little aortic valves, so delicate, so dedicated to the cause. I felt sick, sick as a dog, sicker.

My financial arrangements with Copper have always been, shall we say, fluid. I was fortunate in that when he attended university to study (the *Michael row the boat ashore years* as I remember them), tertiary education was free, more or less. He lived at home and naturally paid no board. When he and Corinne married they moved in with us until they found a small graffiti-daubed flat on which I could afford to pay the rent. It seemed the best, in fact the only solution at the time, and Hester agreed. It was an unhappy time. Family troubles are meant to tighten the ties that bind. I didn't find this to be so. My relaxed attitude to our only child's marriage irritated Hester, though I can't think what else I could have done. On the other hand, her pathetic attempts to "get closer" to Corinne seemed to me a waste of time, effort and spirit. Until Poppy Esther was born, when Hester redoubled her efforts and was rewarded by opportunities to babysit.

New babies seem to me to be as unattractive as newly hatched birds, though the beaks do add an extra macabre note. A few days after Poppy was born she clutched my forefinger in a minuscule fist. I felt weak at the knees, trusted and trustworthy as an insurance company's advertisement.

I felt, although I hesitate to say so, chosen. I was Poppy's man.

When Corinne departed with the now four-year-old Poppy to live with her new lover Marty, I was bereft. We all were, but there seemed little reason, either financial or otherwise, why I should continue to pay for the flat. Our sad son came home and has remained so. This seemed odd to me. Why didn't he, as they say, "Get on with his own life", as if he could get on with anyone else's. I had no objection, in fact I quite enjoy his presence in a vague sort of way, and so does Hester, though not vaguely. But I felt, as I say, puzzled. Why didn't our son find some nice girl and settle down with her. Not to put too fine a point on it, was he not missing out on the pleasures of intimacy.

I assume he has made some alternative arrangements. I hope so, not as an ex-clergyman's son but because, as one of Copper's pop idols used to wail through the walls of the house, he might be *missin' a whole loada fun*. However, the joys of connubiality, to my mind, run deeper than lust.

It was Hester who suggested he should pay some board. I am not sure how much. She calls it her egg money, a memory from her Southern youth when her mother sold eggs from the farm. A large sign screeched EGGS above an honesty box at the gate. I wonder if there are still such things now, the boxes or the honesty.

"What do you intend to do this time?" I said, trying to keep my concern at the imminent collapse of my plan to enchant Hester from my voice.

"Art History."

"Ah."

"I have always been interested in Art. Did a couple of units years ago."

"Yes. Caspar Friedrich. Strong verticality."

"There's one thing though, Dad.

I looked into his eyes. Saw it coming.

"You know you have to pay back student loans now."

"Yes."

"Crippling. Especially at my age."

"So I imagine."

"What I wondered was . . ."

Oh damn and blast. "You want me to help?"

"If you would." He hesitated a second. "Could. It wouldn't take very long. I can cross credit from my previous degree."

The airiness, the God-given airy-fairy thistledownness of it all. I shuffled my feet a bit, bounced about.

"Ah yes. Cross cred."

"There are masses of openings now for an MA in Art History: curators, galleries, valuing, advising clients. There's a new thing now, I saw in the paper. A diploma, or something, which combines Art know-how with business skills. That's exactly what we need. Art as a career in New Zealand is just taking off. Any moment soon it'll be on a roll and I'll be there."

"A roll?"

Years ago when Copper sought holiday jobs from advertisements in the paper he was convulsed with mirth at the ones headed "Suit self-starter". Even then I had not laughed.

"Or I could fall back on teaching."

"Teaching is not a profession on which one falls back."

There was a certain unease about Copper now. A nervousness I didn't like to see.

78

He is my son, I love him. I will help him. But the timing, ah the timing could not be worse. What about my plan for Hester?

"Or counselling," he said. "Part-time."

"I think that would be preferable," I said, draining my second whisky. "Who counsels the counsellors?"

"What?"

"Let it pass."

"You know," he said leaning forward with a confiding smile, his hands around his empty glass. "It's wonderful to talk to you like this, Olly. I can remember when I was a kid I'd come into a room and sometimes, if you were there, you'd get up after a while and walk out." He gave a confiding laugh. "I suppose you couldn't think of anything to say to me."

I said nothing.

"So you'll think about my . . .?"

". . . Request? Yes, certainly." There must be some intelligent phrase I could offer. I glanced at my Pulsar. "Where on earth's your mother? She can't still be at Upholstery."

Copper yawned, stretched his legs. "Yeah, she must be having a heavy session with Jose."

"What? Oh yes. The upholsterer."

"He gave up the classes a couple of years ago."

"But . . . What do they do then? On Thursdays?"

Copper yawned again, heaved himself upright. "I don't know exactly. Spanish, I think. Thanks for the talk, Dad. Night."

CHAPTER
SIX

I went up to bed immediately, almost scuttled through ablutions, teeth, etc., though I omitted the usual flossing in my haste to get into bed and sham sleep, to put my head under the pillow and die. I didn't know what to think. How often we say that — well, some of us; those impregnable to self-doubt have no such qualms — but the worn phrase makes sense to the rest of us. In fact my case was worse. I was unable to think at all, the cognitive mechanism seemed to have foundered under the shock of Copper's languid revelation. All I could understand was that Jose (second name unknown) had given up tutoring Upholstery classes, had presumably had enough, had shoved off home, put his feet up and relaxed until it was time to entertain my wife every Thursday night from that day forward. Why, for what unimaginable reason, would Hester spend two and a half hours per week or longer with an ex-Upholstery tutor of Spanish extraction. Learning the language, Copper had mumbled. Huh!

Something surfaced in my scrambled mind. I remembered that Upholstery had always ceased during the school holidays. A good thing, in Hester's opinion, as she didn't want to miss a minute of Poppy's time with us. Yet now the Spaniard was available on Thursdays, she had no qualms about missing Poppy or anyone else. How could I have not noticed her absences? I suppose because nights with Copper plus Poppy were a treat as different from our usual cantankerous evenings as calm from chaos. We took turns choosing the food. Poppy's choices were as foreign to me as Japanese blowfish; her chicken nuggets, instant noodles, tomato ketchup and pneumatic saveloys were a challenge, I admit, but it didn't seem to matter, and I knew my turn would come in the form of largesse from the new delicatessen nearby called Cuisine Without Compromise: my subtle artichoke hearts, my strong smoked oysters, my tins of *pâté de foie gras* and *confit de canard*. And Copper did an excellent steak.

We were meticulous also in choosing the entertainment afterwards, mainly games dependent on sharp observation which Poppy invariably won or jigsaw puzzles in which she also shone. Copper and I had little to do but bask.

When I said "Huh" I do not mean, or I hope to heaven I don't mean, that Hester has been flagrenting around. I would trust Hester with my soul's core. It is the fact of having such an unworthy thought which is so alarmingly out of place. Of course I trust her. The whole thing is ridiculous.

By this time my mind was thrashing about like an inflatable dinghy in a Southerly buster.

I sat up, took a firm grip on myself. Why was I rolling about, snivelling into the connubial bed like this. If I was concerned I should challenge Hester — no, not that either, more a casual loving mention of the topic: "Copper tells me that you are learning Spanish from your erstwhile Upholstery tutor. That sounds interesting. Tell me more, my darling, my love, my dear heart."

Phoney, phoney as a two-bob watch, and sickening to boot.

There was another reason why I wanted to hide. Tonight was to have been the night when I took my wife in my arms and offered her the treat of a lifetime.

The contrast was too great. I rolled away from Hester's side of the bed determined to sleep. To relax, relax, relax again. Cornwallis, the little window where the sun came creeping in at morn, slipped into the mind. Was discarded. To hell with it.

Later, when returning from a dimly lit visit to the bathroom, I saw Hester's shape beneath the blankets. My wife was in situ. A place for everyone and everyone in their place.

I realise I am no longer a young man. I know that — nature tells me, as do unexpected shop windows. It is some years since Poppy first climbed on my knee for one of her more sedate games called Southern Alps, which consisted of her pushing the slack on the back of my hand towards the thumb, whereupon the folds of skin piled into minuscule mountain ranges. They didn't last long, but the wrinkled hills of time were quite impressive for a second or two.

So I am aware that to the callow and/or callous young, my agitation might seem laughable, to have a touch of *The Miller's Tale* about it. Certainly Hester is younger than I, and my sexual expertise is not quite what it was; although, as I mentioned one night to the accompaniment of her strangled giggles, I hoped normal service would be resumed as soon as possible, I was by no means sure that this would occur. I dislike the thought and I'm sure Hester does too. The fact we have had a pretty good run seems little comfort, although there are other ways to enjoy each other, to give and receive pleasure in an old bed.

But is that enough? Of course it is. Hester, after all, is sixty-five, and my head is splitting and how in the name of all that's merciful can I disembroil myself from this mess.

Hester rolled over. "What's the matter?"

"Nothing, go to sleep."

My last glance at the bedside clock had showed 02.30. The next one was 08.03. My early morning cup of tea, placed on my bedside table by Hester, was cold as a frog's belly.

I attempted a leap from the bed, staggered slightly and clutched the bedhead as she appeared at the door bearing toast.

"Heavy session last night?" she asked.

Copper's identical words, plus the bluest of blue nights, stopped me in my tracks.

"I haven't time for that, thanks," I muttered. "I'll have a shave and run."

"Don't be silly, I'll drive you down."

I gave a sickly smile and headed for the bathroom. Her offer produced another problem. I had not encouraged Hester to visit my rooms over the last five or so years. Quite the reverse in fact. I had even stooped to indicating that my good friend Miss de Lillo was something of a dragon and liked to run her own ship without any interference from the home front as it were. Hester had laughed and replied that she thought Eloise was rather a honey and what on earth was the matter with her? I need not have worried. With her usual lack of fuss Hester had accepted my slanderous statement and continued to do the surgery laundry, send flowers from her garden, attend to the magazines and cleaning arrangements, and more or less leave it at that.

My rooms are within walking distance from home but some distance from the centre of the city. They offer no popping-in benefits for her. The reason I have more or less barred Hester from the place is that I don't want to worry her. The less she sees of the present day-to-day working arrangements at the surgery the better. As I have already said, I have been cutting back my practice for some time. What I have not mentioned is that the practice has been doing likewise.

Periodically I have a session with my accountant, a rapidly ageing young man called Cashem. A nice man, if rather depressing with his talks of "overheads", "imminent threat of running at a loss" and, most alarmingly, "lack of cashflow". There have been moments when I have had to restrain myself from attempting to cheer the man up.

Up till now the cashflow aspect has been good enough to slot in with my master plan to delight

Hester. But that was before last night's chat with Copper. Now my plan shows every likelihood of being shot down by his request for financial assistance. Quite a classical Greek tragedy, this drama. Father's plan to demonstrate devotion for wife unwittingly destroyed by unwitting only son. Nevertheless I'm determined my thwarted attempt should see the light of day. A proffered gift is not as good as a received one but at least she will know I have tried.

The first thing I have to do is to make alternative arrangements for my talk with her. The matter is urgent. I must find a venue other than home in which to tell her of my aborted plan.

From memory I have only two patients this morning. Not enough. The surgery is definitely off limits.

"Hester," I said, as she swung the car into Thorndon Quay, "would you like to have a cup of coffee at The Tulip with me this morning?"

Her look was brief, naturally, but I caught a glimpse of the hidden mirth I had seen early last evening. Her expression reminded me of Poppy's when planting a whoopee cushion.

"Is that the place next to you with the turgid vanilla slices?"

"I'm not sure whether they could be called turgid. White icing."

"White!"

I tried again. "The melting moments are very nice."

"I'm glad to hear it. But why, Olly?"

She drew up outside the surgery and looked at the bright red, blue and yellow tulip shapes sewn on to the hessian curtains, at the tinny little vases on the tables, each with its three artificial tulips, then turned off the ignition with some force.

"If you want me to drop whatever I'm doing at eleven o'clock and drive down to this twee little dump for a disgusting cup of coffee . . ."

"I keep hoping it'll get better."

". . . you will have to tell me *why*."

I took her hand from the gear lever, turned it over and kissed her palm. "I want to talk to you."

She gave an odd little squeak and leaned over to peck me on the cheek. "Very well," she said. "My love to the dragon."

I warned Miss de Lillo I would not require a NATO Standard at eleven as I thought she might be concerned at even such a minor change. Miss de Lillo, like me, enjoys the quiet pleasures of routine. However, she seemed happy at the news of what she obviously regarded as a romantic interlude. There has been something decidedly skittish about Miss de Lillo's behaviour of late, one could almost call it frisky. Very odd.

Despite the trying nature of what I had to relate, I was looking forward to our tea and buns. An old couple enjoying each other's company can induce interested glances, including those from the young. I suppose they wonder what on earth you're up to.

I leapt to my feet to kiss Hester. To my delight she was wearing her old golden tam. "Good God, that must be forty years old."

She pulled it off and ran her fingers through her springy hair. "I thought it might be appropriate."

I could have put my head down on the cleanish red square of table cloth and howled, howled for her perspicacity, her God-given kindness. She looked around The Tulip with its endless coloured photographs of tulip gardens, acres upon endless acres of reds, yellows and pinks. An occasional church spire rose in the distance, otherwise there was nothing to relieve the no-holds-barred tulip panorama.

"Cor," she whispered, "do you think they're mad about tulips or did they just think they would form an easy décor?"

She thanked the sulky-looking waitress who delivered tea, began pouring, topped up the pot with water, fiddled about with milk, then took a bite of melting moment. Crumbs flew.

"Not bad."

"I told you they were good."

She took my hand. "You did, and you were quite right too. Come on, tell me."

I had made a note of headings but I kept it hidden. My first query was not going to be easy. How, or worse why, do you ask a wife of forty years who she was with last night.

I leaned back, brushed crumbs from my jacket. "I hadn't realised that José has given up teaching Upholstery."

Goodness knows what Hester had been expecting to hear but obviously this was not it.

Her forehead wrinkled. "José," she said. "Why are we talking about José?"

Why indeed. I gave a light laugh. "I thought you went to Upholstery classes on Thursday nights."

"Oh, that was years ago." She peered into the pot. "What on earth is this tea?"

One thing I did deserve was her attention. "Hester," I said, "what do you and this José man *do* on Thursday nights?"

"He teaches me Spanish. I told you that years ago."

"No," I said with an authoritative snap. "Never."

She leaned forward, gave me her full attention at last. "Olly, I've been wanting to talk to you for some time about this sort of thing. Incidentally, what's happening to your patients? This will take some time."

"Routine X-rays," I lied. "Miss de Lillo is in charge."

Hester was getting annoyed. I could see the signs, the tightening of the mouth, the brightening eyes.

"I've told you endlessly about my Spanish lessons, or tried to. I try to tell you about the things I do, and time and time again you nod and say, 'Ah yes,' and you go on reading the paper or doing your crosswords until I could kill you. You don't hear a word I say and then you behave as though I have committed some indignity."

I knew I must let indignity pass. In fact I sensed I was on shaky ground. Had there perhaps been some whisper, some talk of José's change of occupation? Spanish, wasn't he? Yes, definitely Spanish.

Hester is talkative, not a bore, quite the reverse; nevertheless she is the type of person who talks to strangers on holidays. I have no objection to hearing her news but I can't swear I have always given it my full attention.

"I think the word you wanted was impropriety," I heard myself say, "not indignity."

She snatched the handle of the teapot. I ducked instinctively.

"I prefer indignity. Now listen to me. You're sweet and funny and a nice man but you can't do people. You have no people skills."

"People skills?"

"Yes. Some people have them in industrial strength. You have none. Or very few."

"We don't all have to," I said with care. "Lots of people don't do people and why should they? Look at Kant."

"What about him?"

How did it go exactly? "His brother who lived in the same town," I said firmly, "wrote to him suggesting they should meet. Kant answered years later saying he sent brotherly thoughts but he was too busy to meet his dear brother at the moment."

"His brother would be Kant as well."

"Yes, but not *the* Kant."

"No," she said. "Some poor sweaty old dud Kant with no words."

The silence was broken by the explosive roar of the coffee machine hooshing itself into action.

The tulips on our table were blue. All three of them.

The only hope was to start again.

"I didn't mean for a moment to intimate that there was anything untoward about your meetings with José," I said. "I trust you implicitly, darling."

I don't often call Hester "darling". I have nothing against the endearment, it's just one that doesn't surface readily.

As I have said, Hester takes things easily as a rule. "Then why are we having a heart to heart in this dump?" she asked.

Heart to heart. How beautiful that sounds. I took her bony little hand in mine. It clenched for a moment then relaxed.

"It's the lack of communication," she said.

Oh Gawd. I'm with Tom Lehrer. If someone can't communicate, the very least they should do is shut up. However, it was now or never.

"I agree I may have missed the information about the Spanish classes," I said.

"And I know it's a cliche," she snapped.

"Please Hester, you'll interrupt my chain of thought."

The chain of thought which concerned me was this. How was I going to get across to Hester the wonder of my plan, albeit now threatened, without admitting to my so-called lack of communication. When women mention lack of communication a man of sense will head for the hills. The phrase, to a woman, is taken as a *carte blanche* to detail any inadequacy in their spouse's behaviour since day one.

I straightened my shoulders. "How would you like to go overseas?" I said.

Her hands flung together, a child confronted with blazing birthday candles. "Overseas!"

We have had holidays through the years, and by and large they have been reasonably enjoyable. When we were young, like most of the impecunious, we saved money by staying with our parents. After a time it didn't seem worth my paying my fare to the South Island. Each to their own, I thought, though Hester was happy to come to Cornwallis at any time. Copper, when he was old enough to indicate a preference, opted for the South but Hester was a meticulous sharer of relatives.

Later we went for what my father called tours of pleasure, not that he had risked one himself. We rented motel rooms, we visited the Art Deco buildings in Napier, the glowworm caves at Waitomo, the thermal pools of the North and the scenic wonders of the South. Hester and Copper have bounced up and down in seas the length and breadth of the country. They seemed to enjoy it.

We went to Australia. I was glad to get home. Overseas, as in Europe, had never cropped up. Maybe the thought of English relatives had alarmed me.

"More tea?" I said.

"No." She stared into my eyes, her own positively snapping with excitement. "Where?" she whispered.

"Britain, of course. Where else?"

I watched the sparkle fade. "Oh."

"*Oh?*" I said.

"It sounds, well, yes, it sounds wonderful of course, but why?"

"God in heaven, I wish you wouldn't say *Why* to everything I suggest."

"Yes, I do see it must be irritating." She picked up the golden tam, tugged the little tab in the middle and shoved it in her pocket. "But why *now*? You loathe travelling, you know you do, except to the States. Why this sudden decision?"

"I wanted to give you a treat."

"Oh Olly. How wonderful. But why Britain?"

Because I hadn't thought of anywhere else. "I thought you might like to find your roots," I said.

"Yes, I would of course, though Doug and Norma looked up some cousin of Snow's near Loch Ness. The scenery was wonderful and they loved a three-piece suite of antlers and Royal Stuart tartan in a shop window, but there was not much Auld Lang Syne apparently. All they knew about us were sheep and earthquakes."

"But what about Copland?"

Hands clasped. "Is he coming too?"

"No, no, no."

"Oh, you mean the village. I thought they were all dead. We had a lawyer's letter, remember."

"I think Decima is still with us, isn't she?"

"Surely not. That was in the letter, years and years ago. She'd be over a hundred, for heaven's sake. But there might be others."

"Who?"

"I don't know, I gave up when you got bored with Christmas cards. You'd better write," she murmured. "Like Kant."

I smiled, rather a sour one, I'm afraid. This lack of excitement at my plan saddened me.

"I would love to go anywhere, of course," she continued, "but somehow I feel I have a nodding acquaintance with Britain. And the scenery's too tidy. I'd rather go to somewhere entirely new. Different. Turkey perhaps, or Greece, or Spain."

Hester, like Copper, dislikes watching pain, let alone inflicting it. She touched my fingers in what I thought was a gentle touch of apology.

Which was also an appeal.

"I can't tell you how much I long to go to Spain."

"With José, I suppose?" I muttered through clenched teeth.

"That would be bliss, wouldn't it? But Olly, you would explode. You hate everything about travelling, you know you do, and there'd be strange people talking funny wherever you looked and no routine and weird food."

My attempt to hide my rage in heavy irony had failed. I dislike losing control, but as Poppy would say, I blew it.

"You'd hate Spain," I shouted. "If you think England's too tidy, Spain would finish you. It's the most untidy, messy dump of a country in the world."

"How on earth do you know?"

"Father told me. 'As for Madrid,' he said, 'you can keep it.'"

"I didn't know he'd been there."

He hadn't as she very well knew. Any more than he'd been to Portugal.

I looked around for some diversionary activity — a coat to adjust, a paper to fold — but there was nothing but blue tulips and me and a disappointed wife.

I couldn't let things go on like this. We were by no means finished communicating, hadn't indeed started. I decided to be brutal, to get the farce over, to shoot between the eyes.

"I had been planning for some time," I said, "to take you on a trip to a country of your choice. As you say, I am not a traveller by nature. I may have been remiss in not suggesting a trip before but the thought had simply not occurred to me. I myself am perfectly happy here. This is my country, here, where Copper accuses me of attempting to make a little England beyond the Seas. Did you know that?"

Her mouth twitched. I seemed to have taken a crash course in noticing, as well as in the risky minefield of communication. I charged on.

"I have also become aware that I might not always have given enough thought to your happiness. I am very fond of you, Hester, and I may have been remiss in not making this more obvious. I apologise sincerely. I will review the financial situation. Peter Cashem may be able to come up with something, though God knows what."

To my horror she burst into tears, her shoulders heaving, her head buried in her arms on the crumb-strewn red cloth already damp from her sobs.

How could anyone, let alone Hester, cry like that. And for God's sake why?

"Sweetheart," I said, "what is it?"

"Don't be so nice to me," she bawled.

We left soon after that. The session had terminated abruptly — we were both worn out. I didn't enjoy my vanilla slice in the afternoon much either.

"Was that lady your wife?" asked Tanya the sad waitress as she slammed the slice down with the tea.

"Yes," I said, anticipating enthusiasm.

Tanya nodded, sucked her teeth and departed looking more miserable than ever.

Apart from the fact that tears terrify me, I could not help wondering about the phrasing of Hester's plea. Why on earth should I not be "kind" to my wife of forty years? The phrase itself worried me. I didn't like it.

I decided that as my attempt at oral communication had foundered in this dire way it might be simpler for me to write a letter. I have written very few letters to Hester. It brought to mind Miss de Lillo's Dear John letter. I heard her singing "Bluebird of Happiness" slightly off-key this morning as she tidied the waiting room. I don't think I have ever heard Miss de Lillo sing before. A little more of this bonhomie and her behaviour would be positively roguish.

My thumbs pricked. Something odd was going on, both at the rooms and at home. I sat at my desk and wrote an attempt to explain how I had not been nice to

Hester, in fact quite the reverse. Having offered her pleasure, I would now take it back.

Dearest Hester,

Have I ever told you that I think Hester is a beautiful name and it suits you well? I apologise for writing this letter rather than talking things through with you, especially as it is never a good idea to commit one's emotions to paper. However, our conversation this morning seemed to run in parallel lines with no prospect of their converging. Also I fear I may have bundled you out of The Tulip rather precipitately but, as you know, I "don't do tears".

To summarise —

1. I was unaware you were taking Spanish lessons from José.

2. My plan had been as follows: —

(a) I had proposed to sell my practice, which Cashem seems to think would be a good idea. I am sure that given its position so near to town and the excellent state of its equipment it would fetch a good price.

(b) I had envisaged Copper staying in the house to keep an eye on things, mail, lawns, etc., while we were away.

(c) However, Copper told me on Thursday night that he wishes to give up his career in WINZ to study History of Art at Victoria University. He also asked me if I would pay his tuition fees. I gather, though I have not discussed the matter with him at any length, that he intends to be at university for some time to get all the qualifications available to him. Also, he feels he might as well have the money now rather than later.

I take his point.

The matter of university fees is not insuperable, but I can't help wishing that he had finished his tertiary education at the time when it was free or almost. He will of course continue to board with us. All things considered, our tour of pleasure may have to be postponed for some time.

3. Would it be possible for me to meet your friend José?

4. Why did you wail "Don't be nice to me" at The Tulip? This may be the most important point of all.

I remain your devoted husband,
Olly

I read the letter through. It was not until I had finished that I realised two important points.

Point A. My father had supported me without comment during my six years at Dental School in the forties. Admittedly fees were infinitely less then, but Charles Octavius, a minor solicitor in Cornwallis, was less than wealthy. So much so that when he died Cashem and I could see no alternative other than my mother coming to live with Hester and me. With her usual dreamy good sense, however, Amelia survived Charles for four months then died drinking a cup of tea in the sun room.

I had accepted immediately the fact that I must pay Copper's fees, but I was pleased to have my resolve stiffened.

Point B. What I had not taken in, or not in the full beauty of its flowering, was that the situation as it was now, i.e. *husband's plan to delight wife scuppered by son's financial needs*, gave me back not only my routine and peace of mind but also credit for unearned generosity from Hester. After all, as they say, it's the thought that matters.

And all in one go, what's more. I was elated. Not only had I achieved my cake and eaten it, it had been handed to me iced on a plate, free, *gratis* and for nothing. The weaving together of so many seemingly unsatisfactory threads of fate into such a satisfactory fabric left me breathless. Copper had saved me from trauma and travel, he had wrapped me in peace and tranquillity. *We were unable to go.* Added to which my slow-beating heart appeared to have transformed itself, from Hester's viewpoint, into a big and booming one — one given to grand gestures of benevolence and unselfishness, one prepared to spend money and time, to suffer tedium or worse, in order to give pleasure to loved ones. And yet, and yet . . . I want her to be happy, to go to Spain, do I not.

I have already been rewarded by Hester's extraordinary tears of what I can only assume was gratitude. Her "Don't be kind to me". Copper also will be pleased and, I hope, happier. I wished I could somehow include Poppy Esther in the equation.

Another thought. I will buy Poppy an Easter Egg when the time is ripe. A big flashy one, pregnant with smaller clones within. Miss de Lillo will post it for me. Should I perhaps buy her an egg as well. On second thoughts, no. This is not the moment for exuberance in any dealings with Miss de Lillo.

I had considered posting my letter to Hester but that seemed ridiculous. On the other hand, so did handing one labelled *By Hand*.

She was setting off on her walk when I arrived home — anti-gravity boots, woolly hat, large smile. I thought she might have suggested I accompany her, but to my relief she didn't. Think of stumping up the hill with the letter burning a hole in the pocket as I waited for the right moment to hand it over. No, the day had had enough dramas already.

Even finding a suitable place to leave the letter at home was not easy. I wanted her to read it immediately so that we could relax and enjoy a glass of wine together while I basked in a glow of, what shall I say? Just a glow. Any old glow would do.

I looked around the sitting room for a suitable spot, admired her pottery vase of dahlias, noted the basket of fine linen and coloured threads required for her Danish cross-stitch. I placed the envelope on top of a half-finished cloth (the Little Mermaid this time, tail unworked). After a moment I snatched up the envelope and put it on the seat of the chair on which she usually sits.

It lay there, a significant white rectangle on the chintz, blinking and winking at me like a friend in the know.

"Hester," it said, *"By Hand."*

Too much fuss, I agree. It was not as though I were leaving home.

I was assembling the Sauvignon Blanc, corkscrew and glasses in the kitchen when she reappeared.

"Wine," she said. "Good. Why?" she said, and ducked her head to my shoulder in mock shame at yet another query. "I've had the most brilliant idea. Olly, it's so kind of you even to think of us going overseas when you know you'd hate it, but then I would too if I knew you were miserable, and it would be so obvious, wouldn't it? Why don't just I go? Save half the price?"

"Alone?"

"No, that's where it's so smart. If you could pay for my ticket I could go with José. He's been saving for months for a trip home and I would so love to see Spain."

She looked at me, laughing, happy in her ludicrous display of innocence. Could anyone ever be so witless. I went to pick up the tray, my hands trembling. Holding on to the back of a chair, I said, "Perhaps it's time I met your friend José."

"Yes, of course, I've suggested it before, remember? I haven't mentioned the idea to him yet. Not till you've thought it through, given it the OK. What do you think?"

CHAPTER
SEVEN

Think. What does she mean, think. I don't think, something's jammed.

I marched back to the sitting room, gave a brief nod in the direction of her chair. "I think you should read the letter I've written you."

She gave me that hesitant look which I have seen too often lately. "Letter? Why a letter?"

Unanswerable. I handed her the envelope.

"Oh," she said, taking it without enthusiasm. "How exciting." She ripped open the thing and read. At last she looked me in the eye, her voice solemn, even a touch stern. So much so that I found myself blinking.

"Yes," she said, "Copper's told me he's not happy at WINZ and yes of course you must meet José and I've no idea why I cried. Perhaps it was a combination of gratitude and shock."

"Shock?"

"All right, surprise. And I do see that now is not the moment to spend up large. But apart from that, what on earth would you do if you stopped working?"

"I would retire. Have fun, hail fellows, make whoopee."

"I do love you," she said, though not with passion. More an expression of friendship towards a slightly dotty aunt. She unwound her legs and came to sit beside me on the only comfortable sofa in the house, one so old it had escaped resurrection. "The thing is, Olly, I've had another thought."

"Ah."

"I could use my money from Dad. Snow Hope's rainy day stash. But that would still mean leaving you and Copper here alone, wouldn't it?"

"Yes."

"Yes. And Copper tells me Corinne thinks he should have more input into Poppy's upbringing."

"That was the word. Yes. Input."

"Input, output, pick up, drop off, as if the child were a parcel." There was passion in her voice now. Over-emotional and misguided and plenty of it.

"Poppy is dearly loved and she is by no means the only peripatetic child in the country."

"*Peripatetic.*"

"Nor is she dropped off, she is . . ."

But Hester had gone, tripped over the sewing basket and stormed out still clutching her letter.

I was upset. Hester has never been one for storming anywhere. She would calm down, of course; she is not a sulker and never has been. And I was sorry, truly sorry her travel plans had been thwarted and she was disappointed, but what could I do.

I took a sip of Sauvignon Blanc, swallowed it quickly as I heard her running downstairs. She appeared for a second at the doorway, waved the car keys, cried, "I'm going out," and disappeared.

Not good, not good at all. No wonder I dislike communication. Whenever I attempt it, relatives burst into tears or storm off.

I had just decided that I would leave the remaining half of the bottle to share with Hester later when Copper appeared at the door.

"Where's Mum?"

"I don't know."

"Odd." He poured wine into the untouched glass.

I leaned forward, interested, paternal. "Tell me, Copper," I said, "what are your plans as regards your increased input into Poppy's parenting?"

He sat beside me on the old sofa in the place warmed by Hester. "Yes," he said putting the basket to rights and folding the half-stitched mermaid. (Copper, the ex-flower child, is tidy in small ways.) "Left in a hurry, did she? Hey, this is good." He checked the label on the bottle. "Why are you drinking it all by yourself?"

Having discovered the wine's credentials he began swirling it around in the glass accompanied with strong sniffs, then rolled it in his mouth with attendant grimaces; even the swallow took time.

"Ah yes, Poppy. Yes," he said. "As I told Mum, Corinne says she has enough on her plate with Marty's two and she has decided I should have more input into Poppy's life." His look was as solemn and stern as his mother's. "And of course, I entirely agree."

Oh, the games we play. Why do we do it, but how could we stop. I can read Copper as a pilot reads a chart and I suppose he thinks he can do the same with me. He wants me to disagree with his last statement even though he has made it in good faith. He wants me to rage against Corinne's decision; any comments from me as to shunting or dumping or irresponsible behaviour on her part would be welcome — he could then berate me for my lack of understanding, could use me as the whipping boy for his frustrations. Yet I know, and he knows, that he and I and Hester and doubtless Corinne and the little kids all want the best for our Poppy Esther. I declined to berate.

"Quite," I said, glancing at his unattractive knobbly bare feet and averting the gaze. "So what solution have you come to?"

His shaggy auburn head lifted. "Simple. Poppy comes here for the school terms and goes north in the holidays, depending of course on what suits Corinne and Mart."

"Quite."

"I thought you liked Poppy," he snapped.

"I do."

"Well then?"

How amazing life is. A brief "Well then" from Copper and to him the situation has resolved itself, has drifted away as mists slip down mountain valleys and melt away.

"Have you considered whether this might be a bit too much for your mother?"

"Mum? She's raring to go. Mad keen."

"She's not a young woman."

"Of course not, but she's fit as a flea, and the school round the corner's as good as ever, I hear."

Another problem solved.

Copper glanced at his watch. "Mum's probably shot down to the supermarket. Forgotten something. Does it all the time."

I am driving too fast and I know it. I am speeding along, passing everything in sight, wishing I could take off like a rally driver; could sail through the air till the spine-crunching jolt of contact, then scream through the dust and fling the car at the turn and slip into the skid, sliding sliding till no one can watch another second and it's the commercials.

People are tooting, and let them. Speed is the thing, to get away, to slam out of Thorndon. On and on and then it's the red lights and the brakes screech just in time.

Stop this nonsense. Now.

And I do, and reason returns and I am sweating with fright. What a fuss. A stupid stupid stupid fuss. A balls-up in B Company, as Snow would say. I'm not even sure, as I fade to my usual speed, why I'm so enraged. My one certainty is that I'm heading to Hanson Street to see my friend José. To talk things over.

I should have rung first. José and I meet strictly by appointment. He has his own friends as I have mine. Joyce, for example, and Heather. We could have a surprise party: Bring a Friend.

"Heather, this is José."

"How do you do?"

"And his friend Jake."

"Nice to meet you, Jake."

Then what?

A truckie in his mile-high cab alongside acknowledges my snort of laughter, waves as we part at Wallace Street, and I think of August '81 and me screaming abuse at Olly as I turn and run to catch the marchers. I knew he wasn't a coward even as I screamed. Of course I knew but that didn't stop me screaming. People are different, you see. Different strokes for different folks, another saying often used by Snow, who is dead and I wasn't there when he died and I hate it. I don't know why, he wouldn't have known.

Serene as milk pudding once more, I pull up beside José's workshop where he lives. I have never enquired as to the legalities of this arrangement. Are you allowed to run your business from your Newtown residence? I neither know nor care.

The picket gate hangs from one hinge, the concrete path is cracked and broken, cerise-flowered weeds romp. A blackbird sings, a cat sleeps out its secret life, a baby cries.

José welcomes me with kisses. "Hello, Mrs Perkins. Come in, come in. Good. Now you will meet my friend Jake."

Bother.

Jake, yes well, Jake is large and tall and tanned and beautiful. He wears a white T-shirt and black leather trousers which creak. He takes my hand, presses it lightly and drops it.

106

"I am going now," he says and does so.

All José's friends, or those I have met, have been so good-looking you assume they must be gay. José is not beautiful; he is animated and intense and vigorous and speaks several languages. We have started on Spanish. He is my tutor and friend, my confidant; we talk together, have conversations which are a rare and beautiful pleasure, where you can agree to disagree and not be maddened by difference of opinion, or not often. It is an interesting relationship — mine and José's — an exchange of thoughts, a breadth of friendship and a growth of, how shall I say, the need to meet again. The necessity.

Snow used to drive once a month to meet his friend Jock Marsh at a pub halfway between Balclutha and Gore. Their wives disliked each other. I asked him why it was worth the effort, why he bothered. He said it was because Jock was the only man he knew who didn't bore his pants off or talk bullshit or interrupt every four minutes. Also Jock was sound, he had his head screwed on.

José turns, gives me his full attention. "Why have you come now, Mrs Perkins?"

"I had to see you."

José smiles, friendly but noncommittal. "Yes?"

"Have you saved enough for your trip home?" I ask.

"Nearly. A month, two months. In not much more I'll have it."

"How would it be if I came too?"

I see his mind ticking. José has a mobile face, his emotions are visible; surprise is followed by interest and dawning pleasure. He decides it would be good, his mother would be delighted, the whole family would welcome me, he could show me all the wonders of Espagne, not the tourist traps . . .

"I want them too."

"And what does Mr Perkins say?"

"He wants to meet you."

"Of course."

"But it's not going to work."

"Then why tell me? How cruel. To tell me yes then say it's no."

"Yes, I know, I'm sorry, but I had to tell someone."

"Of course." He pats my behind in friendly salute. "I am honoured. But why is it not going to happen?"

"Our granddaughter is coming to live with us. Yes, yes, I'm delighted, but I can't leave them alone for three days, let alone three weeks."

"The cooking you mean?"

"Not only that, the being there."

"Jake is a chef."

"Oh José, don't be silly." I kiss his cheek, taste the pungent smell of roll-your-owns.

We drink a sherry at the kitchen table. He can't afford Spanish and the local is so bad, he says, that we must drink it with ice to cut the pain. I find it agreeable. He will think of something, he says. I will be the perfect travelling companion.

I think of Poppy and wonder when she is due to arrive. I couldn't leave her of course. Not for a minute.

★ ★ ★

Hester appeared home an hour later, calm and bearing news. She dropped a kiss on my forehead and told me that José would like to meet me. She had obviously cleared it with the Pontiff and it was all systems go, just when I had formulated the comforting thought that I wouldn't have to meet the man, there being no point, now the plan had foundered. I was glad to see Hester, quite apart from the fact that the fragrance flowing from the casserole in the oven was making its presence felt. It had that cooked smell about it.

"Thursday," she said, "we're to go to José's next Thursday."

This was no moment to carp. I nodded. "Thursday."

Hester stopped the car. I peered at decrepitude through misty rain. "Is this it?"

"Yes."

My eyes blinked. Hester has told me I do this when I'm nervous. She may well be right. I asked if we had an umbrella.

She said No.

I climbed out, disturbing a pair of copulating cats. I found myself tiptoeing around the screeching heap in tactful silence. They disengaged, one disappeared up the alley, the other strolled away snapping the end of its tail in dismissal.

The door opened. A slight figure in jeans and a black sweater appeared beside a man twice his size.

"Everything happens at once, doesn't it?" said the smaller one, putting out a hand. "I am José Mendez and this is my friend Jake who must leave us. Mr Perkins, Jake Starke, Mrs Perkins you know."

"Hi," said Jake, flicking his gum to the other side as he creaked his way out. "Gotta go."

I stepped out of his way. The back of his black T-shirt was stamped CREW in white. A handy man in a shipwreck.

If there is one thing I dislike it is uncertainty, social, economic or emotional. What is my role tonight as regards my host? Had I come to inspect the man's credentials? If so, how? Should I perhaps ask to see his passport? And where would that get me.

We shook hands again, why I don't know. José was unexpected. He is, for one thing, homosexual, or so I think. A man of average height, dark eyes, curly hair, friendly. The main impression he gives is one of vigour and intensity. His jeans, his jersey, his face, his fluffy hair are all, as Copper would say, well presented. I wished Copper was there. I longed for his casual approach to life in general and awkward moments in particular. He sails through bad quarter-hours with the heroic idiocy of a white butterfly. I needed my son.

My social unease was partly because I felt a fool. But why did Hester not tell me of her friend's sexual persuasion? It had undoubtedly put a different aspect on the situation. My over-reaction, my sleepless night had become risible.

On second thoughts, I think I know why Hester did not tell me of José's sexual proclivities. José is her true friend; she trusts him as I trust Miss de Lillo. If the latter were to become a Sapphist it would be her

110

business, not mine. After all, her affection for the NATO Standard cousin may have been a girlish fling before she found her true self. However, I had still no reason to rejoice at Hester's keenness to abandon three generations of her family to visit Spain with the man.

José's workshop-cum-living space could be described as neatness under pressure. The goods awaiting repair were cumbersome, the tools of his trade bulky. Presumably he slept behind the dark curtain at the rear which must also hide the cooking arrangements. He showed me to a chair awaiting attention which gave me a vista of upended lounge suites, a couple of what used to be called occasional chairs, and a disembowelled sofa. I found the sight soothing, a busy workshop where work, and good work too, was done, though I wish I could suggest that he lighten up on the padding. I wondered if José learned his trade at home or here, not that it matters. Presumably upholstery skills travel well, belonging as they do to a trade where command of the local language is not as vital as in some livelihoods. You just grab the davenport and start banging — little communication is required at the workface.

His tools lay on a workbench alongside; tack hammer, staple gun and more specialised pieces of equipment labelled Bar Clamp, Stuffing Regulator, Foam Saw, lay neatly alongside each other on the small space.

"José," Hester murmured, "is a perfectionist. Everything is tidy, even the ceiling." We looked upwards to stare at the bolts of cotton padding, horse hair and webbing stored in rows among the rafters. She lowered her eyes, patted a wheeled office chair. "This one is going to be recovered in leopardskin chenille, can you believe?" She laughed with the haughty smirk of the insider.

José joined us, laughing as he handed wine. "Kinky, eh?"

My slight empathy for this place and its occupant vanished. I was filled with irrational irritation. Why should my wife have shared upholstery jokes with this man without my knowing. I saw them last Thursday night, heads together like small boys swapping gum as they chuckled over the louche choice of fabric for a whizz-about office chair, inventing scenarios to explain reasons, while I was being berated with strong words and dull food by Copper in the kitchen at 59.

It was not that I am interested in upholstery — anything but. No, it was the intimacy of their shared knowledge which annoyed me.

I knew I was being ridiculous. Jealously often is. Previously, however, I had found that its pangs become less sharp with age. Not many seventy-five-year-olds commit *crimes passionnels*, although like most things there have been exceptions.

Many years ago I learned a defuser for this miserable waste of emotion. I devised a method of damage control. It went like this:

If I envied José I must envy him *in toto*: his job, his surroundings, his blisses and his woes.

Which I don't. Ergo envy disappears.

Or that is the theory.

I touched Hester's hand.

There was no coercion to meet José this time. She had merely smiled, told me that of course I must meet him. Of course I must.

I have never thought of Hester as a particularly determined woman; the idea of her getting more so as she ages alarms me, quite apart from the fact that the end product of her determination is entirely for her own ends and pleasure, which again seems unlike her.

I felt that Hester was behaving like that other loyal spouse, Penelope, who wove her tapestry by day and unravelled it by night in an unlikely ploy designed to keep her unwanted Ancient Grecian suitors at bay, her agreement with them being that she would not choose a new spouse from the importunate bunch until she had completed her tapestry. Her secret agenda (Copper again) being that during these delaying tactics her husband Ulysses would reappear and put them to rout, which he did.

Hester dreams up equally unlikely master plans which would enable her to get to Spain with José and yet somehow avoid abandoning Poppy to the sole care of Copper and me. And by sole I mean just that. Even Mrs Chaytor who used to help out once a fortnight has gone to Gisborne to help Raewyn with the trips.

Every morning Hester, having dreamed solutions all night, wakes to tell me that plan X has unravelled with the dawn. It won't do, she tells me. She will just have to give up the idea. It's not possible, even with Snow's money which she knows he would want her to spend on something she has longed to do for so many years.

I never understand why sensible people can make categorical statements as to the wishes and views of those who have passed over the great divide. The whole point, it seems to me, is that such people have no thoughts, no wishes, no views. They have ceased to be.

Certainly Snow Hope was a decent man and loved his daughter. If he had been asked when in good health and with his wits about him, he might well have said he would want Hester to spend her inheritance on travelling to Spain with a Spaniard about whom her husband knows little other than a fact that he has a heavy hand with the Stuffing Regulator and gives Spanish lessons on request.

Snow made no such statement on the matter, that is my point, and it is too late now. I find nothing morbid in this thought, though it is one I would hesitate to bring up in mixed company. Snow Hope, like many others, was a good man and did good things. He will rest in peace. A glorious conclusion in my view.

Conversation, presumably Spanish, was continuing between Hester and José, who were now sitting on a small green sofa which had lost its innards and sagged; was in need of stomach stapling. José, the true surgeon, would have to Go In. This was no cosmetic tinkering about with nips and tucks; this was in the nature of a rebore.

One result of this sag was that gravity had rolled Hester and José close together; she was practically perching on his knee as they talked. As always with a foreign language, their unknown words sounded important and exciting. Hester could even have been asking him, though it was a slim chance, to remove his knees from beneath hers. Or not.

I once heard a woman in a Greek restaurant in New York screaming at a chef with what I assumed was loathing until she turned to me, smiled and said, "They *will* overdo the onions." One needs the lingo.

No. Undoubtedly I should not go overseas. Britain would be foreign enough, Spain a farce.

I was becoming bored. Soon I would be counting the rolls of stuffing above my head. We were not getting anywhere. I swallowed a yawn as Hester smiled at me.

"José is going to make us a paella," she said.

"Ah."

José beamed his attention on me. "I understand from your wife that you are a gourmet, Mr Perkins. Knowledgeable about good food. Ah, you should come to Spain."

"I have never thought of Spain as one of the great culinary experiences," I said with faint coolness.

José became even more fervent. "Ah, but you have not been guided."

I had realised the man was intense, but obviously I had underestimated him.

"Food," he cried, flying his arms wide, "good Spanish food is my life."

"How do you manage in Wellington?"

"As any gourmet should do," said José, now laughing, chaffing, backing and advancing, "I cook my own. A few things Madre sends me from Madrid — saffron, for example, is a ridiculous price here."

Otherwise, his palms flew upwards to tell me, life was a cycle of song in the Spanish cuisine of Wellington.

"Olly's favourite food is offal," said Hester as if this explained something. "Anything that has had to be excavated. Except ears, of course."

This set José off again. The Spanish, especially the Madrilenians, love offal. There is a delicious stew made from the entrails of chickens, one of the few offal delicacies he finds difficult to obtain ingredients for here. Other delights he can knock up with ease — the homely *cocido*, a stew cooked with chickpeas, beef, marrow bones, bacon, hot sausages, saffron, golden thistles. (*Golden* thistles.) Or *Callos a la Madrileña*, tripe, he tells me as I have never been blessed to meet it, with blood sausage, pieces of ham, garlic, red peppers, spices and God knows what. And the sucking pig — José's lips kissed bunched fingers, hands flung again in rapture. The hams. Ah, the Andalusian jam'ons hanging in the wine bars.

"Don't they drip?" said Hester.

"Of course, but —" José demonstrated "— they have wee cups."

She gave a puzzled nod as José sailed on. He told me of the pleasant Spanish habit of offering food to strangers. It is bad manners, he said, for Spaniards to eat or drink without sharing.

"No one is a stranger in Madrid. Its inhabitants love their city, they like nothing better than to show its joys." Last time he had arrived in the train from Paris, as the lights of the city appeared the whole carriage leapt to their feet shouting "Madrid". He himself had had tears

116

in his eyes. People reacted as though they had been offered free wine. Everyone waved, laughed, cried. Madrid is not the most beautiful city in Spain, he admitted. No, Spaniards love it for its bustle and gaiety, its *animaçion*. José assured us the euphoria of the city comes from its inhabitants, the light-hearted sons of Madrid. People call from their balconies to their strolling neighbours, they dance in the streets at fiestas, they love the whole world. "They speak loudly and ver' ver' fast," he told us, snapping his fingers. Ah, how he misses the markets, the haggling, the selecting, the sampling.

All of which confirmed my suspicions. Good offal possibly, but the thought of being offered food by a loud Madrilenian steeped in *animaçion* and hellbent on welcome, no. Thank you, but no.

Madrid, it appears, is a place for people persons, not for the Perkins of this world. A thought confirmed by José's summing up. When he is home, he is lively, exhilarated, he talks to everybody, he goes to bed late, he overeats, he sits for long periods in café terraces watching the world go by. He enjoys life to the full.

Hester was staring at her language teacher as though he were offering a state of beatitude, an unexpected nirvana to be obtained not by the extinction of individuality and desires but by the reverse. Madrid could be said to have been made for her. I looked at her lovingly. She is after all a people person. She would enjoy Spain. I wished she could go.

I took her hand, felt tempted to kiss it but didn't.

"Unfortunately," I said to José, who having refilled our glasses with a rather nasty red was now rolling himself a cigarette, "there is no possibility of my being able to go to Spain but I do wish it were possible for Mrs Perkins to do so."

I left it at that. A true statement.

Whether I wished it were possible for Hester to achieve this with José I was not so sure. He seemed a pleasant young man, late thirties, early forties, but the fact remained that I knew nothing about him except that he was unlikely to want to make advances to my wife. There are, however, other virtues one would wish one's wife's travelling companion to have. I had to find out more. Was he trustworthy, honest, efficient as to all those "travel arrangements" which, speaking personally, thicken the blood. To be frank, the fact that Hester, determined though she is, would never desert Copper and Poppy and me in favour of Madrid did make life a great deal easier, though not for her. I did see that. So the very least I could do for her, having made an attempt to make her happy and been thwarted by circumstances, was to maintain the myth that she might conceivably go. I was here to meet José, to learn more about him, and the obvious question to ask him tripped off my lips.

"Thank you, José, for such an interesting exposition, but would you tell us why on earth you left?"

José's face puckered; he looked dejected but beguiling, one of those monkeys with a ruff of hair around its lugubrious face.

Spain, it appears, has a negative side. There is apathy, ignorance, indolence, sometimes a sense of hopeless fatalism. Misfortunes are put down to *El destino*. *"Es le vida,"* they say when they discover they have bought a house above an exdump. José snapped his fingers. They cracked in my face like a small charge.

He himself is not like this. He would move the house, clear the dump. Something, something would he do. Would I believe what his poor father did for a living? He was a coat beater: customers brought him their winter coats to be beaten and stored in a special anti-moth room. "From nine to one my father drummed the coats, and again from 4p.m. on. The sound is with me still."

The siesta of course remains sacred. From two to four the populace sleep. Every attempt to legislate working hours from nine to five has failed. "When I was young a politician tried once more. He was laughed at, called the Abominable Man of the Nines."

"Oh," said Hester.

José was spluttering with mirth. "In Spanish the word for nine is *neuve*. The word for snow is *nieve*. Instead of calling him 'The Abominable Snowman', they ridiculed him, called him 'The Abominable Nine Man'. It is a joke, see?"

Hester and I laughed.

"You see?"

"Yes. Yes, of course."

"I myself," continued José, "I am active, hard working; I get up and go. Also I am not interested in large female bottoms. I had to get out."

I let this comment pass. What else could one do with it.

"But why New Zealand?" I said. A country not noted for its *animaçion*, which is one of the reasons I like it, though I kept the thought to myself.

"Ah, that was a happiness," said José, "a good luck story for me. Two of them. One, I was apprenticed to an upholsterer friend of my father who also worshipped at the Shrine of the Big Behind and his only pleasures were sleep, wine and admiring female bottoms with his old friends. The older the man the larger the one he admires. It is very strange. And another important good luck thing. My sister Teresa married the son of an Otorohanga farmer, who was working with her in a café on the Plaza Mayor."

"Married and gone to New Zealand," I said.

I thought of mentioning that Elizabeth Barrett Browning had written that, but there seemed little point. Whether EBB meant it to or not, the statement has a sense of finality about it. My mother would have liked it.

"Yes," said José.

"And you followed?"

"Yes, and never have I regretted it. However, I find it essential to go home every so often."

"To top up your *animaçion*."

José was delighted at my wit. Soon we might be *simpatico*.

"It is such a pity Teresa's marriage broke up," said Hester. She has always dropped me little conversational

120

hints like this. I regard them as kindly offers to assist the conversationally impaired.

"Oh dear," I said.

"Yes," said José. "Drew was a snake in the grass."

"Ah."

"They lived forty kilometres into the ooloo but that didn't stop him having a floozy in Otorohanga near the Kiwi House."

I was beginning to like José again. His English is excellent and he is rightly proud of it. He has that fluent use of idiom and the occasionally squiffy use of the colloquial which I find attractive.

"Mind you," he said, "Teresa told me that it was not so much Drew she missed as the farm life, the space and the sky and the hills and the hard work. And the animals. She is like me, Teresa, a real little goer. Drew is a lazy gringo which is worse than a Spanish one — at least the Spanish manage to look as though they are enjoying themselves when doing nothing. The only thing that woke Drew up except the floozy was the electric fences. Perhaps he was making atonement like my great grandmother and her hairshirt."

"A real hairshirt?"

"Oh yes, she wore it every Lent, I believe." His voice dropped. "I wonder what happened with it."

I sat waiting for help from Hester.

"Teresa is a dear," she said. "You'd like her, Olly. She's a chef in a downtown café, the El Toro."

"Again it is hard work and rents are . . ." José demonstrated: "Pouf. Fortunately she has a night job with my friend Jake, you saw. Yes. Jake has a small business."

He handed me a card:

JAKE THE FIREMAN
and his
FLAMERS
Let's make your party
SIZZLE!
Reasonable rates
Call Jake for details
(04) 385–8494

Hester was no help this time. We could be discussing a new dahlia. I had to know.

"What do they do?"

"Oh, Jake does a real raunchy strip, and then Teresa and Ces — that's the other exotic dance lady — they do a spot of discreet stripping for the boys. The helmet and all Jake's stuff make a good gimmick. He bounds in, sort of clanging all his gears. More of a contrast, if you like, when he gets down to it. It's very tasteful, isn't it, Mrs Perkins?"

Hester considered. "I'm not sure what an untasteful one would be like," she said finally. "But yes, I found it interesting."

Interesting, she says. I have no wish to see this performance, but to think that my Hester, so pure in mind and deed, should have seen this exhibition, given it her appraisal and not mentioned it, astounded me. But then I thought, No, she would say that she did tell me, that probably I hadn't been listening, then she'd kiss the top of my head and say, "Bed darling," and we'd climb the narrow stairs and bed it would be. All of which is real and worth a lot.

I looked at my love and attempted a smile. "When did you see this performance?"

"Oh, I haven't, but Jake and Teresa and Ces came round one Thursday to discuss the idea with José and did a sketch to give him some idea of what they were after. Jake brought his helmet, for example. I must say it seemed a bit odd at first but then I could see that really it was just an extension of those ghastly Gorillagrams, you remember, Olly? And wasn't there a Singergram and something to do with cakes, or did I make that up. I can see it would fill a niche at parties which sort of, you know, needed something. Not twenty-firsts perhaps, but I could see Jake the Fireman could give some parties a little tickle-along. And he has a most beautiful body, hasn't he, José?"

"You can say that again," said José, topping our glasses with a flourish.

"Apparently," Hester continued, "Teresa and Ces don't strip — well, not entirely. Yes, it's unusual, but I can see it might have its place. It's going very well, the business, isn't it, José?"

"Very, like a bomb." He leapt to his feet. "Jesu, man, I forget the paella."

He dashed behind the curtain; we heard clattering, banging and loud Spanish cries which made Hester laugh. He reappeared. "Fortunately she was all ready to go. I should have asked Teresa, she is a better chef than

123

me. Her paella —" He kissed his fingers once more. "Hester knows Teresa and her paella."

It is odd how observant I have become since life's dramas increased. Hester's and José's eyes locked across the length of the warehouse, they communicated, they agreed. "Teresa," they breathed in unison. They smiled.

"Paella," I whispered to distract her. "How long does it take?"

She smiled. "Not long."

Jesu, man.

CHAPTER
EIGHT

"The paella was good, wasn't it?" I said as I took the wheel.

"Delicious," said Hester, her voice equally casual, her other life still as unknown to me as that of the fluffy-legged cat which shot across the pedestrian crossing in front of us as I slammed the brakes. How did the weird-looking thing know I would stop. How did it know I cared.

Hester smiled at me, gave me an approving animal-lover's knee pat. Approving ones are even worse than other pats, but again she does not know this. Perhaps I could tell her my secret dislike to even things up. Trade José's existence for my distaste of knee-patting. No, the odds are wrong; no one would stake my puny little cave weta of a secret against her slumbering moa. No contest.

To hell with it. I was tired. Hester was tired. She patted me, we kissed, we slept.

The balm of the morning routine soothed me as usual. I enjoy the walk to the rooms, especially on mornings such as this when the grass around Old St Paul's has been newly mown. The rustic smell pleased me as the polluting traffic trailed nose-to-tail alongside. Quickened by pedestrian smugness, I lengthened my stride until stopped in my tracks by the sight of an old bike frame outside the deconsecrated porch door. It was an eyesore, a skeletal excrescence dumped by an idiot, which must be removed. I turned in through the gates to do so, to take it round to the back of the church where someone in a position of authority could deal with it before the Japanese tourist buses swept up to debouch.

Halfway through the gates I stopped. This was not for me. Someone else could deal with it. Besides, if I were caught moving the skeleton, questions might be asked.

There is always something to distract the worried mind, but regrettably not for long.

Miss de Lillo continued to be frisky. I had been giving her time, hoping that she would calm down. After all, everyone has ups and downs, although there seemed to have been an excess of that sort of thing going on around me lately.

She greeted me with her usual wide smile. "Guess what, Mr Perkins?" she cried. "We have a new patient."

I was pleased but refrained from showing it. New patients, I wished to demonstrate, were peanuts to Perkins.

"Oh," I said, "what is the name?"

"Menzies," said Miss de Lillo. "Miss Menzies, she said."

"Ah."

"That makes four this morning."

126

I nodded and walked to my desk. Huh, I thought. Yippee.

It was time for some good news. Life, or rather its complications, seemed to have been conspiring against me lately. And all this thinking lark — one can see the phrase "cudgelling the brain" has stayed with us. Thinking about one's problems is damn hard work, takes up a lot of time and, so far, doesn't seem to have got me anywhere. *Qui bono?* as the Romans so rightly said.

Miss De Lillo asked me if I were free to take a personal call.

"Hullo," said the voice. "It's Debbie here."

"Debbie?"

"Debbie from Books 'n' That."

"Of course."

Debbie of the golden navel.

"I found a box of cryptic crosswords from the UK out the back and I thought I'd give you a buzz."

"Debbie, that's wonderful . . ."

"Yeah, well how many d'y want then?"

"How many books are there in a box?"

"Thirty."

Thirty would undoubtedly see me out. On the other hand, if they're slow sellers and there's no call for them they will probably hang fire for some time.

"Fifteen, thank you Debbie, and I'm most grateful . . ."

"Yeah, OK. I'll put them aside."

"How on earth did the box get missed?"

"Happens all the time," said Debbie. "Lucky I took your number, eh?"

And thus it is, and thus it is that life brightens. Not from a meaningful finger from on high, but dropped casually by a disinterested but amiable child with a tanned midriff. God moves in mysterious ways. When he wants to of course. Debbie took my number and I am glad.

And Miss Menzies as well. Perhaps she too was a sign of better days, like the song of the shining cuckoo we used to hear in the spring in Cornwallis. *Dah, dah, dah, dah, diddley pom* he used to sing, and again I was glad. Some indigenous flowering species do it too. The first star-shaped flower of *Clematis paniculata* appears on a small stand of native bush and next time you look a canopy of white has spread from side to side.

I am not a superstitious man but it would be nice to think that Miss Menzies could be a forerunner of other patients beating their way to the surgery door. The first shy petal, as it were.

Miss Menzies, though by no means shy, was an attractive woman, under forty, small, with a tumble of black hair and what I tend to think of as Mediterranean legs — well-developed calf muscles and slim ankles. Local Greek and Italian ladies have them and now Miss Menzies, and very nice too.

She stood on her toes to shake hands with me and told me in an accent I could not place that she had come to me because her brother told her that Mr Perkins would not hurt a fly, and that she, Miss Mendez, not Menzies at all, was a coward about dentists and was it true that I am skilful in avoiding pain?

I put her fears to rest and asked her brother's name.

His name was José Mendez and she herself had gone back to her unmarried name. She had left her husband who was a no-hoper from Otorohanga and had I heard that Spanish ladies are very open, they say what they think.

I am not given to flashes of insight, or used not to be until I met Denise in the Echocardiogram Unit and all this fandango started. Now, however, I do have these blinding flashes, and quite alarming they can be too. I saw Hester's and José's eyes lock once more at the mention of his sister Teresa and her ability as a chef. Add that to Hester's steely determination to get to Spain come what may, and it occurred to me that Teresa Mendez's appearance in the rooms was unlikely to be coincidental.

I asked Miss Mendez to get into the chair, remembering as I did that I must enquire later into Miss de Lillo's hearing ability. Menzies? Mendez? Possible, I suppose. Accents are gargled by telephones.

Miss Mendez's teeth were in excellent condition, her smile as dazzling as that of a television news reader. I told her she had no caries, however it was wise of her to come for a checkup, and would she like me to clean her teeth while she was here?

Miss Mendez gave me another flash of teeth and a glimpse of a rounded calf as she hopped down from the chair, thanked me but declined my offer, shook my hand once more and disappeared to be followed by

129

Miss de Lillo with my NATO Standard. She stood pink and hesitant beside me and asked whether it would be convenient for me to have a word with her or should she come back later.

"Why not now?" I leapt to my feet. "You sit here and I'll take the Planmeca."

Miss de Lillo became pinker in protest. She must sit in the Planmeca, I must stay where I was. So there we were with my coffee cooling by the minute as we continued our insistence as to who should be uncomfortable.

Miss de Lillo won. Her hands were clasped, her eyes anxious. "I really don't know how to start," she said.

I smiled, though I was distinctly apprehensive. We sat looking unhappily at each other. I reached for my coffee, then remembered it is impolite to eat or drink in front of others in Spain and put it down, thought bugger Spain and picked it up again.

Miss de Lillo told me that her cousin John, from America, the NATO Standard one, had retired from the Defense Service in the USA. His wife had died and he had expressed a wish to come to New Zealand to renew his friendship with Eloise de Lillo, view matrimony, and she was sorry because she felt her going might leave me in a bit of a hole. On the other hand, she felt she should let me know how the land lay, although of course neither she nor John would be rushing into anything. But then again you could never tell.

Miss de Lillo, my friend. She has a heart of gold and horselike teeth, even to the worn-away enamel on the lower jaw which reveals the dark line of dentine within. Usually this is found in pipe smokers but not entirely. Perhaps Miss de Lillo is a tooth grinder.

I leapt up again, took Miss de Lillo's hand and shook it warmly. I considered kissing her forehead but refrained. I continued shaking her hand up and down and wished her all possible happiness and told her she must not worry herself in the slightest about her replacement. Someone will turn up, I said, my heart lurching and my feet cold. I knew Mrs Perkins would join me with my congratulations, or rather felicitations for a lady isn't it, and what a pity we couldn't lift a glass but how about I took her to lunch at The Tulip instead.

Whereupon Miss de Lillo flung herself against my clean white uniform and told my desolate soul how wonderful it was and she didn't know anything.

We shut up shop early. I went to pick up the cryptic crosswords from Books 'n' That. Debbie was off sick. I left a message of thanks for her, and mooched home. No pigeons at Old St Paul's.

Hester was back from her walk. She kissed me, then held me at arm's length as though checking for jam on the face. Then kissed me again.

"Did Teresa Mendez come to the surgery today?"

I knew it.

"Yes."

"What did you think of her?"

"Amiable, good ankles. Rather Spanish of course. Perfect teeth."

"Oh good. Did she tell you she was José's sister."

"Hester, what is this nonsense? If you think I would allow a young woman of the type I believe is known as an exotic dancer to take over the household, teeth or no teeth, while you're away and Poppy is with us you must be stark staring raving mad. And who's going to pay the bill for her examination?"

No answer.

"I agree the term 'exotic dancer' could cover a large range of activities," I continued, "but that is the whole point, don't you see, a loose term which could include any reasonably young woman ranging from an apprentice belly dancer to an in-the-buff professional. Euphemism is all in the sex industry, naturally enough.

"Similarly the word dance can be used in the widest sense — from a sort of wiggling or grinding motion to the complete immobility insisted upon from the show girls at the Folies-Bergères, or has that ceased now? As always America has the right words for the process — 'striptease'. Is this the sort of exhibition you would let your seven-year-old grandchild see?"

Her face was stern. "Don't be so silly. Poppy's not going to see anything. Everything will work out splendidly and I know Teresa would never do anything indelicate."

"*Indelicate* — huh!"

"Wait a minute, wait a *minute*," said Hester. "She would save on her rent as well as her expenses; she would get a stand-in sometimes for the night job and work shorter hours at the El Toro which they're quite happy about now summer's over. It's only for three *weeks*."

Once again we seemed to be moving in predestined grooves. "Whose bright idea was it for Miss Mendez to come to the rooms? Yours, I suppose. Frankly, Hester, I find that beneath you."

"Like a lap-dance client?" She giggled. "I love it when you go all pooh bah. It was Teresa's idea, to meet you on neutral ground, see you in action as it were. That was one of her conditions. She's very astute, Teresa."

"Conditions. And what was her verdict?"

Hester picked a thread from the sofa and wound it around her finger.

"She thought you were sweet. A lovely man, she said. She'd be happy to knock up a paella for you any day."

"I will not have Teresa in the house with Poppy."

She stood in front of me, my erstwhile easy-going Hester in cut-off white trousers and striped T-shirt, her arms akimbo and legs apart, pugnacious and determined as an eighteenth-century powder monkey.

"I am going to Spain with José. We are making our plans and we're going. I wouldn't go if there wasn't someone sensible, practical and of good character to look after Poppy, but I know Teresa well. I have complete trust in her and you're jolly lucky to have her."

Hester. Hester of all people. And she had won.

"When does she move in?"

Transformation was instant. Hester was in my arms and I was wonderful, noble, talented and sweet.

I freed myself. "I am not damn well sweet. When does she move in?"

"We thought about a week before we leave would be plenty of time for her to settle in."

So we did, did we? Then we fly Abroad, don't we, the two of the both of us, all consciences cleared and free to go, impelled as migrating godwits heading north.

"And when does Poppy come?"

"Oh, you know Corinne. Her arrangements always seem to be in the lap of the gods. I'll ring her tonight."

"Please do."

I picked up my pristine paperback of the *Times* cryptic crosswords and gave my attention to the Across clues. Nothing came to mind. Not one. Impossible. *Depicted with a strange appearance* (3 down, 5 letters). Surely they hadn't changed the composer.

Hester kissed my forehead, murmured "meal" and departed before I realised I had not mentioned Miss de Lillo's news. I tried clue number one again. Useless. I must stop this self-pity. Poppy is coming.

And Hester is going.

And Teresa is coming.

I flung the crossword across the room with force as Hester came in again.

"I thought we might have an aperitif," she said, ignoring the book landing at her feet, "seeing it's a special occasion."

She lifted her glass to me. "Here's to the sweetest man in Thorndon." She sipped, lifted it again. "And to change."

Copper, as so often, was of two minds. He was torn between his support for his enterprising mother and her gay friend José who is a great guy, and his dislike for the general upheaval. Who was this Teresa woman? He was pleased to know she is José's sister. He liked José, but will Poppy like her?

Poppy, as we all know, has views.

I pointed out that it was Teresa or nothing. Mum was going to Spain.

He took my point. "So what does she normally do, this Teresa?"

"Works full time at the café and flats with two mature students."

"So she's young?"

"Youngish." I didn't mention Teresa's night job. I have no views on exotic dancers, being as they are a topic about which I know little except for the fact it takes two to tango and always has. It was only my fierce protective feeling for Poppy that roused me. I want her to grow better as she grows older, not merely know more.

Copper said that he would be so busy working out his plan for leaving WINZ and making sure he got his full entitlement of his superannuation that he would be working on his PC most nights, getting everything tied up. So Teresa wouldn't bother him much.

An alarming thought. Would I be expected to make polite conversation to Teresa in the evenings? This put a new complexion on the benefits of her night job.

Copper had not finished discussing the topic of WINZ. He wouldn't mind dumping a load on that prick Barker in Projects. Couldn't organise a piss-up in a brewery. However, he wouldn't want to get any of his mates up the creek, let alone members of his team. As for Publicity, all they needed was a bit of leadership to get things rolling and they'd be away.

I explained that Teresa would do the cooking and the cleaning and work part-time at the café so she could be home when Poppy came back from school. Also she was prepared to meet Poppy at school if required.

Copper's nod was ponderous. He had been thinking of that aspect, he said, and then reverted to his master plan for the most desirable way to make his departure from WINZ.

Wheels within wheels, he murmured. He would have to get his departure tied up soon enough to leave plenty of time for sorting out his Art History options for enrolling next year.

A statement so obvious I could only blink. I wondered who Copper's team were. I did once glimpse a youth wearing the corporate wardrobe and dirty shoes feeding a shredder in his room. Copper's, I mean. Other than that, I have not seen hide nor hound of a team member, or not to my knowledge.

"They say she makes a good paella," he said finishing his coffee. "Hell, look at the time. See you, Dad."

The pace quickened. Everything, as José said, happens at once or almost.

First came a long letter from a man who signed himself Bernard G. Perkins who told me that he is the son of my first cousin Edmund and thus a great-nephew of Charles Octavius and his ill-regarded brother Lionel (who died of disappointment in the West

Indies, though not according to my mother). I saw no reason to doubt the man's claims. Though I should have thought there could be little benefit accrued in his claiming kin with me. No, the thing which puzzled me was why he had sent it and was his second name Gurth like mine and Copper's?

The next arrival was Poppy, whose plane landed early.

Undeterred by the absence of Hester at the airport, she asked her minder/escort to ring Thorndon. No answer. She then gave her father's mobile number. Whereupon Copper rang me to say he was tied up at the moment and would I fill in? One fleeting thought as to how he could assume that a dental surgeon could cancel his afternoon's list at a moment's notice and I was into the cab. I arrived to find Poppy practising her tap-dancing steps in the dim light from above the still-revolving carousel with its forlorn cargo of two unclaimed backpacks.

She flung herself at me, said this was Serena and could we go now.

I apologised to Serena, a pleasant woman in one of those daft hats and her overnight trundler at the ready. She was in full agreement with this suggestion and departed at speed.

I picked up Poppy's battered grip and looked at her. Thin as a rake in white pants and T-shirt, topped by an oversized red woollen cap of the type favoured by the late Pierre Cousteau, she melted the heart. She reminded me not of Cousteau, however, but of *Amanita muscaria,* that pale-stalked red-capped toadstool you see occasionally growing beneath the pines of Tinakori Hill.

She hugged me again, was glad to see me and asked if I had any new jokes.

The best bit in the flight, she said, was the man beside her who kept yawning and saying "Pardon me" and trying to stiffle them. I suppose she meant stifle but it was a nice attempt.

Hester was home again when we arrived, having slipped into town to pick up her airline ticket. She flung her arms around the child as though she were about to eat her and apologised profusely for not meeting her.

"'s OK," said Poppy, "Olly came."

I should have kept my mouth shut, given an affirmative nod and left it at that, instead of which I heard myself waffling on about a couple of unexpected cancellations, always a nuisance, in fact infuriating, but well timed in this case.

I was shocked to catch the look on Hester's face, a look combining pity and sorrow, the sort of look one might give to an immensely brave patient whose prognosis is bad. A look which shook me rigid. Hester *knew*. Not only did she know that I had lied about nonexistent cancellations, she also knew about the parlous state of the practice, and *probably had done so for years*. How I don't know. Not from Miss de Lillo, not in a thousand years. Perhaps she counted the towels. Rubbish. She knew because she was a perceptive woman cursed with feminine intuition and was sorry for me. Damn and blast and bloody hell. So what now? My attempts to spare her from worry seemed antediluvian, fit only for an Edwardian child bride. I couldn't return her gaze, and anyway she'd turned her face away. All I knew was that the heart had hit the gut once more and things were worse than ever.

Poppy had headed immediately for what remains of Copper's old toys now housed in a dilapidated shoe box (gents size). She was followed by Hester who knelt beside the child and explained that she would be away for three weeks.

Poppy glanced up briefly. "Who will cook our dinners?"

"Teresa will be here," said Hester. "You haven't met her yet but she's very nice."

Poppy had discovered a new Lego pack and had time only for a brief nod.

"You must ring your Mum," said Hester. "Tell her you're safe and sound."

"Yeah. The little kids'll be missing me. Wait till cheap rates, though eh?"

"I'll go and start the meal. Do you want to help me, sweetheart?"

"No thanks," said Poppy, tackling Lego on her stomach.

"Poppy," I said after a while.

"Yeah?"

"It's all right Hester being away, isn't it?"

"Yeah, sure."

She snipped a few yellow blocks together and kept her eyes down. "Dad'll be home soon, won't he?" she said.

"Yes."

"Cool," said Poppy, and grinned at me.

I didn't enjoy the surgery either. Miss de Lillo crept around, her mouth pursed with melting compassion until I could have kicked her. Any more anguished glances and I'll join a circus and take Poppy with me. And Hester knows the practice is crumbling and still she goes to wretched Spain which is what I want her to do but *how does she know?*

I must get in touch with Cashem.

The next crossword book was also useless.

Hester was full of praise for Teresa from the moment she arrived. She was so quick, so bright, she caught on immediately, though she'd need a little help with the dishwasher which was on its way out. And so pleasant, nothing seemed to faze her.

"Good," I said.

So here we are. Happy Families one and all and a pretty peculiar feeling it is too. Teresa the little flower is tucked up in the rose-patterned spare room. She insisted on taking over the household immediately rather than treating this week as a shake-down cruise, which she told us is a sailor's term for a trial run to see if the thing sinks, or that's what Bill said anyway.

"Who's Bill?" said Poppy, who seemed to warm to her immediately.

"Bill's Bill," said Teresa, "and I thought I told you to brush your hair before tea."

So Copper and I are at work, Poppy is sampling Thorndon Primary which she tells us is "gud". A lot of things in Poppy's life are gud. I can only hope this is true, rather than evidence of a limited vocabulary.

I don't know what Hester does with her unexpected spare time. She is loving, almost shy with me, presumably to prepare me for her absence. She has stopped gazing at me as though I were on a long waiting list for urgent surgery. She is also particularly loving with Poppy, but her granddaughter is still dazed with the joy of being with Dad once more, to which Copper responds with wit and alacrity and affection. He springs out of chairs, he leaps to greet, he hugs, he is a different man; almost, in fact, a happy man.

Teresa made us paella on Hester's last night. I drank too much and fell snoring into Hester's arms the minute we got to bed. Or so she told me, kindly, next morning.

We farewelled them *en famille*, we farewelled them endlessly at the airport. Teresa came too because of José. They hugged, they wept, they spoke Spanish, they embraced again while Hester and I held hands as discreetly as possible and my heart sank. That dull sense of impact, as if a previously inflated object has collapsed in the pit of the stomach.

It was difficult to think of anything to say. Even Hester was silent.

"I hope everything will be all right," she said eventually.

"Of course it will."

She stared straight ahead. "Yes."

"Oh, by the way, I had a letter from Uncle Lionel's great-nephew yesterday. Bernard Perkins."

"I didn't know he had one."

"Well, there's Copper for starters."

She smiled, rather wan, but she tried. "What did he say?"

"As a matter of fact I haven't read it yet, only the signature. I just thought you'd like to know."

"Yes."

I buried my head on her coat collar and held her.

I told her not to fuss, that we would have a great time and she would too, and if she didn't I'd sue her and it's only three weeks for God's sake.

"Where's Poppy?" she said

Poppy, never a shy child, was chatting up José's farewellers. Jake was there and several other cheerleaders. She sketched a few tap steps.

Finally José offered a courteous arm to my wife and they headed for the Departure Lounge amid cheers from José's supporters. I lifted a hand.

"Which one is Bill?" Poppy asked the weeping Teresa.

"Bill? Oh, Bill, the sailor. Years ago, Bill was. He landed up on the ferries."

She put her arm through mine with simple grace. "Come on, Mr Perkins," she said. "Let's go home."

CHAPTER
NINE

Old wood as well as young can be attacked by the canker of self-pity. It must be ripped out like the heart of an Aztec sacrifice, then stamped on. Stamp, stamp.

It is not only missing Hester, it is the lack of routine. We have not settled into any sort of rhythm since Hester's departure. In fact life at 59 Tinakori Road has become something of a shake-up cruise. Small children appear before I leave the house and have restaked their claim by the time I return. They are active, these little girls, they hurtle up and down stairs, they slide down banisters shrieking. They giggle, they appear in unexpected places and make me jump. Teresa makes little attempt to control them. I can only assume that her ideas on discipline come from the let-'em-rip school of modern childcare. "So long as Poppy is happy," she says, and Poppy is happy as a sandboy. Cassandra and Jade are her best friends and school is cool.

Teresa is also active when I arrive home each evening. She is in housekeeping mode, barefoot and busy with an apron at the waist. She favours an impressive-looking duster made from hanks of wool stuck to the end of a stick which she tucks into her centre-back apron strings. When she runs up the stairs it bobs behind her like the tail of a retreating possum. Rather a nice image, and she has pretty feet, Teresa.

She also has an interesting system of tidying up. Newspapers lie in one pile, books in another, and a miscellaneousheap of everything else lines the far wall of the sitting room. The effect is an illusion of tidiness, a sort of tidiness manqué, achieved with grace and speed as she dips and leaps about like another seven-year-old.

Teresa has one good rule. Any child, be she standing on her head or hopping on one leg or making merry hell, must leave at five o'clock on the dot. This gives Teresa time to prepare our meal and arrange our tapas in peace.

Tapas are the *bonne bouche* of Spain and a delight for the adventurous eater: fried anchovies, small squid, prawns, diced potato with peppery sauce, olives, cheese, the list is endless and I enjoy them all.

I always enjoyed my drink with Hester when she told me the business of her day and I glanced at the paper. Now, however, when Teresa and Copper (who seems to be arriving home earlier each day) talk together I find, for some reason, that I listen to their animated exchanges.

This evening Copper mentions that he might lay some paving stones down the back, make a sort of patio so we could catch the last of the sun with our tapas.

Paving stones? Copper?

144

"What do you think, honey?" he asks Poppy, who is making his hair pretty by plastering the front curls flat with spit.

Poppy approves of the idea; so does Teresa. Conversation becomes technical.

"They're called pavers now," says Copper, adding that he is not sure that the fried anchovies are happy with the wine. Teresa tells him that's because the wine is not fierce enough and we need a rough Spanish red. *Pitarra*, perhaps, or *Maqueda*.

Copper removes a whiskery bit of anchovy from a front tooth. "Anyway, I'll look into it. Get the cost per paver, sizes etc. OK by you, Dad?"

"There is no 'last of the sun' in Thorndon. It just disappears."

Copper opens his mouth to say of course there is but is interrupted by Poppy who, restless and questing as a spaniel, is now rootling in her enormous and expensive backpack for a teacher's note. She nearly forgot. There is to be a Parents' and Teachers' meeting at school on Wednesday and Miss Amber Priddle will be pleased to see as many parents as possible in the school hall from 7.30p.m. on.

"That's the day after tomorrow," says Copper. "You've only been there five minutes, hon. No point in my going."

Poppy is not pleased. He would be a stink if he didn't and she wants Teresa to go as well because Poppy has given a Morning Talk on how she looks after us, and Amber said Teresa sounded lovely and she would like to meet her.

She turns to me, pats my hand and says I could go too as Amber says it's lovely to see the older folk and we must remember to be nice to them all the time because they can't help it.

"Honey, it's nuts," says Copper.

It is unnerving how dark a seven-year-old's scowl can be. Copper, Teresa and I stared at the remains of the tapas.

"Everyone's mum and dad's going, Cassandra's and Jade's and Greta's and Ruby's. I'll be the only one with none."

"Don't be ridiculous, Poppy," I say at the same time as Copper tells her that of course we will go if she wants us to. He looks at Teresa, smiles his beautiful smile and says that although there is no reason why she should come if she didn't want to, we would be delighted if she could. "Wouldn't we, Olly?"

I have no memory of Parents' Evenings. I suppose I went. "Of course," I say. "Of course."

Teresa kisses her hand to Poppy, whose scowl has now cooled to a slow burn.

"Sorry, sparrow," she says, "I'm working tomorrow night."

"What doing?"

"Dancing."

"Dancing's not work."

Then we have a tedious discussion as to what is working and what is fun, and dancing is fun so Teresa could come to the Parents' Evening.

Teresa says Jake is relying on her, and besides she gets paid for her dancing and that's that.

Whereupon Poppy goes into a deep sulk and Teresa leaves us to attend to her *cocido*, and Copper and I make stilted conversation as we attempt to ignore the wretched child, who, like her father before her, can transform within seconds from a competent agreeable youngster to a pain in the aspidistra.

At the table she eats her *cocido* with similar lack of good humour and announces that she is going to hide now and we needn't bother to find her because we wouldn't.

"OK," says Copper.

I do dislike this sort of thing. The irrational swings, the puerile arrogance of the young.

After the meal I sat in a tub chair with another impossible crossword watching four starlings goosestep up and down the braided trunks of the pohutukawa in the front garden. I didn't know starlings could do that. Looking for insects, I suppose. It seemed an odd thing not to have noticed before. Their strutting stride reminded me of the verger at St Mary's, Cornwallis; a nice old man, always wore a green pork-pie off duty.

The tree has a protection order on it because it is of historical interest. Everything in Thorndon is of historical interest. Meanwhile the tree flourishes but refuses to flower and the room darkens and it's all a damn nuisance much as I revere and respect pohutukawas.

We still hadn't heard from Hester.

Teresa and Copper appeared from the kitchen where he had been giving her a hand. Any concern for Poppy's state of mind by her father seemed to have disappeared. Sensible behaviour, I know, but I dislike the thought of the child being unhappy.

Hiding has always been Poppy's fall-back position. I can remember Hester telling her "Big girls don't hide" after we found her last year, but obviously to little effect. We eventually found her under Copper's bed, covered with balls of dust and clutching one of his old jandals. I found the whole thing disturbing. It was the jandal. Such desperation.

"Where is she?" I said.

"She'll come out soon," said Copper. "You were saying, Teresa?"

Teresa pushed back her dark hair and handed him his coffee. "It's just a question of being comfortable in my own body," she said.

"Yeah, I suppose so," said Copper thoughtfully.

"I mean I'm not nude. I wouldn't do nude."

"No. No."

"Or topless."

"No?"

"Sure, what I do wear is pretty skimpy but I'd never go the whole hog. None of that guys tucking ten-dollar bills into G-strings stuff. Jake'd have them out on their ear no time flat. I mean there's nothing wrong with my body, but it's mine if you see what I mean."

"Yes."

"Ces went topless for a while and she's still confused about it. One minute she'd think, 'This is OK,' and then she'd be like, 'Is it?' So she gave it up. It's a question of personality really, of being able to carry it off, as well as the privacy issue. I mean we're all different, aren't we?"

"Sure. Yeah."

"Samuel de Cubber say," continued Teresa, "you know about Samuel de Cubber. Seen the pics?"

"No."

"No? Yeah, well he's a really talented male model in the States. Martial arts, great body, muscles everywhere. Full frontal's nothing to him."

"No?"

"The other thing of course," says Teresa, "is the dosh, but the whole entertainment scene is changing now. People are more open — well some, anyway. On the other hand, there's the Art question. Jake and us girls are proud of what we do, and what he'd really like is to attract the mature crowd who'd appreciate the artistry of the whole thing. He says it's more a case of waiting for people to warm to the idea. And then again, he says, there's all these women in really high heels wanting to shout 'orgasm' all over the place. It'd be like taking the lid off a boiling pot if things went that way. It's just a question of getting the guessing right. A sort of wake-up call if you like. That's what Jake says."

Poppy's head appeared behind the sofa by the window. Her eyes are bright, happy.

"Let's all go and see Teresa tomorrow night instead of Amber," she says, clutching her hands with excitement like Hester.

And now we are all talking at once. Copper tells Poppy it's sneaky to listen to other people's conversations, it is called eavesdropping and is not a good thing. Poppy says, Why? She had told us she was going to hide and why was it called eavesdropping.

I tell her that an eavesdropper is someone who stands underneath the edge of a roof to overhear other people's secrets. Poppy says she doesn't get it. What secrets? And why *not* all go to see Teresa tomorrow night? And so we begin the full nausea once again as we attempt to explain to Poppy that the three of us are unable to grant her request to see Teresa dance tomorrow, and instead Copper will oblige her previous request to go to Thorndon School Parents' Evening.

At which stage Poppy bursts into tears, tells us we're all stinks and she wishes Granny was here.

Yes.

Hester telephoned next evening, almost incoherent about the wonders of Madrid. It would be nothing like as good of course if she were not with José. The kindness of José's family, their wonderful hospitality, their gaiety. "Madrid," she tells me, "is a place where the spirit soars. I've never felt so *alive*, so stimulated. Like New York. Remember? And how are you getting on?"

We all speak in turn to tell her how delighted we are to know she is having a wonderful time and so are we, my goodness, yes indeed.

"There are no problems at all, Mrs Perkins," said Teresa. Copper, his arm round her shoulders, agrees.

"What is the food like?" I asked.

"Very nice," she said, a touch firmly.

"Would I like it?"

150

"Of course."

Poppy gave a friendly word or two to indicate regret at Hester's absence but she has recovered from last night's sorrows and does not mention them.

I took back the receiver. "Goodbye, my sweet, goodbye."

"*Hasta iuego, guapa,*" said Hester.

"What did she say, Teresa?"

"Until two weeks, farewell."

"Nothing else? It sounded much longer."

"It is the endearment, *guapa,* a nice word."

"What's it mean?"

"*Guapa* is like, say, darling."

Teresa is now giving Cassandra and Jade and Ruby and Greta and Poppy rudimentary flamenco lessons, teaching them the steps and the techniques which apparently cannot be learned early enough. Flamenco, she tells the class, is Spain.

Peter Cashem has rung me at work. Would I go and see him. It was not exactly a matter of urgency but he would like to talk to me.

"Strangely enough, I was about to ring you," I said. "Tomorrow?"

"Certainly. Ten suit you?"

"Done."

Cashem greeted me with his usual manly handshake. His face was more worried than ever, his hair creeping backwards in retreat from other people's financial problems. He asked me if I had considered making an attempt to sell the practice. He added that he thought it would be a good idea. I said I had been giving the matter some thought.

I am not normally a pessimist, not by nature one of the doomers of this world, whereas Cashem seems to be getting worse and worse. What did he mean by "attempt"?

He told me (in all honesty) that the practice was on its last legs, thereby combining an image of tottering senility with a flippancy of tone which I disliked. He honestly thought there might be no other alternative but to sell. I asked him what he thought I might get; he said he had no idea but we could only hope for the best. I mentioned the excellent quality of the equipment, the Planmeca Prostyle, for example. He dragged a hand over his tanned face and said he'd always wondered why I had chosen a baby-blue one, but that in any case it would go with the practice. I replied that I had always thought the blue to be more azure than baby, whereupon he looked more miserable than ever and said I might well be right but that his considered advice would be to sell and the sooner the better. He added that seventy-five was a fair age for a dentist to be practising.

I left Blair, Brewster, Cashem & Jupp feeling curiously detached. *Que sera, sera,* I thought. There was little point in both Cashem and me having a breakdown. I would worry about the whole damn thing later. In the meantime The Tulip for a vanilla slice and another stab at their coffee. Tanya the sad told me the vanilla slices weren't out yet but that she could give me a ring when they'd cooled down a bit if I liked.

I declined her offer and strode into the surgery giving thanks for Miss de Lillo. A thought which brought only fleeting comfort.

Nevertheless, her coffee was as good as ever. She told me she had been going through the files so she could be sure that everything was in A1 condition in case anything came to a head suddenly.

I nodded.

"Five patients this afternoon," she said. "That's good, isn't it?"

"Yes," I said and handed her the small suitcase of clean laundry dispatched from Teresa that morning.

Miss de Lillo said she was sorry Ms Mendez had decided not to come back for a good clean, apologised for getting her name wrong, and departed, leaving me alone with my malaise. To have worked hard all my life and be greeted by this. And what about Cashem? Wasn't that his job, to avoid this sort of thing. If he halved his fees we'd both survive. However, apportioning blame was not going to do any good. I must and would concentrate later; in the meantime the trick would be to slip the mind on to something more pleasant.

Teresa, who seemed to be turning into a treasure, came to mind.

Yes, I missed my routine, but Teresa's exuberance interested me. She is brisk; she is, damn it all, merry, and seemed to be getting more so.

She cooked, she cleaned, she sang Spanish love songs; she ran up the stairs with duster bobbing to reappear minutes later clutching a load of laundry —

"To wash," she cried, as if it were a rallying cry, a call to arms from the wash house.

Another thing. She, well, she notices me. Each evening she stands tiptoe, one hand extended upwards to greet me as I open the door. She drills the flamenco squad like a marine sergeant and they beg for more. As for Copper, Copper is lost in a cloud of adoration. Teresa tells him that in Madrid it is considered a sin for a young woman not to make herself pretty. He replies that he can see that, and Teresa claps her hands high and believe it or not cries *Olé*. Copper is behaving like a boiling pot with an ill-fitting lid.

The only visible signs of Hester being no longer at the wheel are the red pubic hairs embedded in the soap in the shower. Normally Hester, Copper and I share this bathroom. There is another mouse-sized one between the spare rooms round the corner which Teresa and Poppy use at the moment, but Copper, like other large men, prefers *lebensraum* when washing and there is access from the hall as well as from our bedroom.

These auburn hairs are not mine. I have never seen them in this bathroom before, so unless Copper has suddenly begun to moult there can be no explanation other than the fact that his mother has been silently removing these intimate by-products of his ablutions for years. Men should not leave hairs. Especially red. I put out an unsullied cake in the hope that he would take the hint, and threw out the hirsute one. Anything rather than a father and son talk. Not straight after Cashem.

154

I have no objection to a friendship between Teresa and Copper. However, once again I have been thrust into the role of Poppy's moral guardian. Not in front of the granddaughter seems to have become my benchmark — a word I am uncertain about. My dictionary tells me it means "a standard, a point of reference", which I suppose makes some sort of sense. Politicians, prizefighters and punks, we all, whatever the reason, have our benchmarks, and mine is the maintaining of Poppy's innocence.

Breakfasts, unlike other meals, have turned out to be a disappointment. I had not been expecting anything cooked of course but I thought there might be some little bakery exotica, small items whipped up in minutes, some kind of flat biscuit perhaps, or puffy little hot bun. Not so. Breakfasts are of little interest in Spain apparently. Coffee yes; otherwise, the only specialty seems to be some tough rusk thing with an unpronounceable name.

"Anyone want a new hot water bottle?" said Copper.

Poppy stopped chasing dry rice bubbles around her plate for a second. "On special, are they?"

"Yeah. At The Warehouse. This yoghurt's disgusting."

"Throw it out then," I said, "and give me a bit of the paper."

He flapped a bit at me.

"Thanks."

"Yeah, I thought those things were defunct."

"Not at all," I said. "They can be a great comfort."

"I can think of better ways to get warm in bed," said Copper, and leers at Teresa.

I blinked with shame at such crassness. Poppy looked puzzled, Teresa all smiles. I understand that Spanish women are, as it were, trained to be flirts (the language of the fan, things of that nature) but frankly . . . Their glances lingered.

Poppy slipped from her chair, climbed on to Copper's knee and stroked it.

"If Olly went to the Parents' Meeting you and me could watch *Shortland Street* and ring the little kids. And Mum. I want to talk to Mum."

"OK," said Copper. "Why not. If it's OK by you, Olly?"

"I have no wish to go to Thordon School Parents' Evening. You said yourself, Copper, it is ridiculous. No."

Six eyes turned to mine, two of them doleful. Why did Poppy want to talk to her mother? Surely she can't be feeling, God forbid, insecure? Why ring Corinne when she is alone with her father enjoying a cosy Daddy-and-me evening in front of the soaps.

"Oh, all right," I said. "Seven-thirty isn't it? You'd better get fish and chips, Copper. Too much for Teresa otherwise."

Poppy thanked me and said she hoped there'd be other older persons for me to talk to.

Copper said he had known I'd go, which irritated me.

★   ★   ★

The school was undoubtedly tucked away. I couldn't even find the place until two likely looking women converged on each other from the shadows.

"That you, Rach? I knew it was. Going where I'm going?"

"Yeah. Tons of time though, haven't we."

"Mm. Who's Jared got this year?"

"Mr Shorter."

"Lucky Jared. So few men in Primary now, aren't there. What about Livy?"

"Miss Harding again. Make you weep, wouldn't it? This way . . ."

I followed but not too closely, coughed occasionally, stamped along, anxious to be recognised as a pilgrim parent rather than a stalker. However, they were now engrossed in the unsatisfactory performance of Leone's swimming coach which lasted until we reached the Hall.

I can't have been here before. Not only would I have known where it was, I would have remembered the smell: the same faintly stale air, the sense of disembodied bodies and limited heating met me at the door. Teachers sat at desks as parents queued to meet them; disconsolate lines of parents doing their stuff waited to be greeted by teachers doing likewise. I wondered if they, the teachers, counted the heads in their respective queues. *Getting along quite nicely, only six more to go,* that sort of thing. Fortunately, Miss Priddle's line was below average in length. No seats, not a glimpse, except a little one for the teachers and another for the supplicant parent at the head of each queue.

Miss Priddle was a healthy-looking young woman with a wide smile, one that seemed to confer pleasure on each parent. Of course she knew Louis. Louis was cute as a newt, especially now he was learning to use his language skills in conflict situations . . . "Mr Bassett is it. Hullo and yours is? That's right, Scottie. Well you couldn't miss Scottie, could you?"

And so she continued, radiating energy and enthusiasm for each and every mudlark in Room 4B.

The only problem being that her interest and delight in each pupil slowed things down interminably. Parents in Miss Priddle's line were not dispatched quickly. Each one was given ten to fifteen minutes to tell and hear all, to receive comfort, advice and praise. Room 4B's queue crawled. I was the last.

She looked up, smiling, as I fell into the small chair in front of her. "And your name is? Ah, Mr Perkins. Oh, so you're Poppy's . . .?"

"Grandfather. I'm known to Poppy as Olly."

"Oh *Olly*," she said, "I've heard a lot about you."

I sat luxuriating in the comfort of my hard chair. "Oh."

"And Dad's Copper, is that right?"

"Yes. I know it's ridiculous to bother you when she's just enrolled but Poppy was anxious that one of us should put in an appearance." My light laugh hung in the chilly space. Some of the teachers were already showing signs of shutting up shop.

Not so Miss Priddle. She looked at me with concern, her plump hands folded on her wee desk. "So why couldn't Dad come?"

It seemed an odd question. I wondered whether Miss Priddle was one of those ever-smiling women whose slightly intrusive questions intrude on your privacy inch by inch until you notice too late it has gone.

"Our housekeeper was unable to babysit."

"Ah," said Miss Priddle, "and her name's Teresa."

"Yes."

Miss Priddle was now more confidential than ever. She glanced around the emptying room as though checking for spies, then turned back to me smiling.

"And she's Spanish, isn't she?"

"Yes."

"Yes," she said, her brown eyes pleading. "And I gather there might be wedding bells!"

"What?"

"In Poppy's Talk. You'd be amazed the things they come out with. She said she was hoping to have two mothers, one of them Spanish and another ordinary one up north."

Out of my depth, floundering, I lifted a friendly hand. "I'm afraid I don't know, Miss Priddle. I assume Poppy has settled down at school?"

"Oh yes, she's a lovely kid. That's why . . ."

I stood up. "Thank you. Well, yes, thank you very much. Now, if you'll excuse me, Miss Priddle, I'll say goodnight and thank you once again."

Miss Priddle was also on her feet. "Oh I do hope it comes off. She'd be so disappointed. They were having fun in the shower, she said. She could hear them laughing."

My sick smile remained friendly. "People do, you know. We will just have to do the best we can, won't we. But don't worry, Miss Priddle. Seal of the confessional and all that."

"I'm not a Catholic."

"No? Well thank you once again for your help. Goodnight, goodnight."

I lurched to the door, took care not to stumble on the steps, remembered to switch on my torch.

All I could think of was flight, flight from Miss Priddle and her presumably well-meant news, flight into the gloom of backstreet Thorndon. Panting a little, breathing deeply, I followed my torch beam home.

How naive of me to think that Copper would have taken my hint as to the extraction of pubic hair from soap. I had had an extra lick of pleasure from my shower in the last few days when I had been under the impression that my tactful removal of haired soap had succeeded, that Copper was finally learning the basics of civilised behaviour. Had been relieved, in my innocence, that no dire reprimand from father to forty-year-old son would be required.

No such luck. He had merely changed showers.

Once again I was embroiled in What to Do. Reprimand was not the right word, but it would do for a start.

I opened the door and marched into the house. Not a soul in sight. The telephone rang briefly as I was hanging up my coat, then stopped. I could hear

Copper's voice: "Hi Mum, good t' hear you. How's it coming?" as I headed for the kitchen telephone. Anything other than talking to Hester side by side with Copper at the moment.

I picked up the receiver. "Hullo."

"Olly darling, how wonderful to hear you. How *are* you?"

"I've just come back from Poppy's Parents' Evening."

"Good Lord," she laughed, "how wonderful. How did it go?"

"Very well thank you. And you?"

"Mum's got some news," said Copper.

"You're coming home early?"

"No, but the most wonderful thing has happened."

"What?"

"You'll never guess."

"Of course I won't. Tell me."

"José has a new boyfriend. Wait till you meet him, he's a wonderful young man called Juan. Lovely the way they met, too. I'll tell you all about it. Fantastic, isn't it."

"Ah," I said, "give them both my congratulations."

"Of course. And how *are* you all?"

Copper burst into a paean about Teresa which went on for some time. "Amazing isn't she, Dad?"

"Yes."

"And my Poppy Esther?"

"Never better," I said. "And you?"

Hester told us. They had been bargain hunting in El Rastro flea market, made a day trip to Escorial —

rather creepy in her opinion but interesting. As for José and Juan meeting. They'd gone to see José's old uncle who kept beehives up a hill nearby. And Juan who lived next door came over to borrow something. Otherwise they would probably never have met and wasn't it wonderful. But then that was Spain, unexpected delights in every day.

"What does he do?"

"Grows oranges."

"Might be difficult to get him a permit to live here."

"Oh he's just coming for a holiday first. See if he likes it."

I put the receiver down, then remembered my duty. "Copper," I called, "I'd like a word with you."

"Now, Dad? I'm working on resigning from WINZ. Seems to have got a bit behind."

"How odd."

He appeared on the landing all smiles. "Yes? Can't think why."

"I want to speak you. Now."

"Oh, all right," he said, clattering down the stairs. "It's wonderful how well Poppy and Teresa get on, isn't it?"

"I wondered whether Poppy wanted to tell you something this evening."

"Spot on. She wanted to tell me how much she likes Teresa."

"Oh."

"Yeah. Like a whisky, Dad?"

"No thanks."

"No?"

"No."

"And how did you get on with Amber Priddle?"

"She told me that Poppy had told the class in her last Morning Talk that you and Teresa are taking your showers together."

Copper gave a baying laugh, clapped his hands. He could not contain his pride and his joy.

"Yeah, she told me that. Great kid, isn't she? Amazing. Just wanted to tell me she likes Teresa as much as I do and she wouldn't mind joining us sometime."

It's true. The mouth does drop.

"Are you sleeping with Teresa?" I said eventually.

"Not here."

"Well don't. And I hope you're leaving the soap clean, no imbedded hairs."

"Hairs?"

"Hairs."

"Oh, *hairs*. Wha'd'y'think I am. Certainly not. Not that she'd give a toss. Listen, here she is." He rushed to the door and began his greetings. Which went on for a considerable time before they came into the room entwined, with Copper, tall as a mast, straight as a bolt, enfolding his lady friend. Teresa disengaged herself to greet me with her usual courteous handshake.

His voice was solemn, his smile ecstatic. "Dad, let me introduce you to the future Mrs Perkins. She says she'll marry me. Us."

Overcome, speechless, his hair flopping, he picked up his intended by the waist, swung her around like a milk crate and deposited her gently in front of me.

"Say hullo to the old man, sweetheart."

Teresa stood on her toes and gave me a butterfly kiss to right and left. "I am so happy, Mr Perkins. And you I hope?"

I was no longer surprised to find myself in agreement. "But why didn't you tell Hester?"

"Oh, I hadn't asked her then. Had I, sweetheart? Just a few minutes ago."

Teresa agreed, looked at Copper with adoring rapture. "I am so lucky, Mr Perkins."

"Let's have a whisky," I said. Teresa, our little flower, opted for brandy.

"I couldn't have asked her before, you see, Dad," muttered Copper as we poured the drinks. "Not until Poppy came clean, which gave me the go-ahead. God, I'm a lucky man."

"Hester, we must ring Hester," I said as the three of us lifted our glasses.

But they were lost, both of them together and alone on another planet.

CHAPTER
TEN

What a performance this flossing of teeth, this oral hygiene lark is. Mouth open wide as a sideshow clown's, eyes starting from their sockets, hairs up the nose. And does it work? I have never found much literature on the subject. Who knows, perhaps it is one more tribal ritual to placate the fastidious and the scared, a token gesture towards sparkling teeth and sweet breath. Hang on to both while you can.

It was not always so. Barry, the bike shop man of my childhood, was given false teeth for his twenty-first. Delighted with the gift he was too.

So, I asked that face, where do we go from here? I can't wait to hear Hester's reaction. It will be no use her saying they don't know each other well enough. A fortnight's proximity in historic Thorndon seems to have been more than enough.

I was pleased to discover how pleased I was, and not only for Copper's and Poppy's sake. Many people will be interested. Corinne, how will she react? Marty and the little kids? Room 4B will be excited, to say nothing of Señor and Señora Mendez and Hester and me. The whole damn family, in fact.

I climbed into bed and shut my eyes to serene and pleasant thoughts which were soon submerged by gloomier ones. The practice. Money. Disaster. Cashem and his Sell Immediately. How?

And what about my promise of support to Copper. He will be married; soon they will have children, dozens of them. What if it won't sell? How do you go bankrupt? What do you do? And Hester knows. Hester knows. Hester knows.

This must stop. Such night terrors lead to madness.

I used to have good dreams: dramatic, erotic, lost in Xanadu with maidens, stringed instruments. Gone, all gone. Just tedious threads remain: dancing starkers at the checkout, whimpering in the maze.

Oh God. I burrowed deeper.

Somebody was shouting, attacking me. I surfaced, no faculties remaining, no sense but rage.

I groped for the light switch. "Whaat?"

"Olly, it's me," cried Poppy, scarlet in the face but shivering. "Listen. There's someone at the front door."

"What?"

She was now in bed beside me, clinging in bear pyjamas.

"Listen," she said again.

"Poppy, what *is* this?"

"There's someone there and no one's answering. *Listen.*"

Faint as a dying echo I could hear something, a sort of ghostly thundering downstairs at O three double O. I grabbed my mangy dressing gown and headed for the door, pursued by Poppy.

"Don't you come, sweet. Where's Dad?"

"I couldn't find him." She slipped her hand into mine.

And he said he wouldn't. Not in the house. He promised.

"You stay here," I said.

"No."

"Well, hide when we get down then."

"OK."

Still holding hands, switching every light on as we passed, we crept downstairs to louder thunder.

"Front door," I said.

"I know."

"Just a moment. More lights." I grabbed the poker from the sitting room. "Now you stay here."

"No."

"Don't be such an idiot." I stormed out, flourishing the poker.

Someone was now kicking down the front door.

A small hand slipped into my other hand.

"Stop it," I shouted and turned on the porch light.

The upper half of the front door contains a small stained glass window, Victorian in colour, pre-Raphaelite in style, rather attractive in a wishy-washy sort of way. In the clear glass between the drooping lilies and the lovers' profiles I could see the blurred shape of a tall man in a hat, which I found reassuring. No one would commit a felony in a hat like that.

"What is it?" I shouted.

"I am looking for Oliver Gurth Perkins," he roared back.

"Why?"

Poppy's hand tightened.

"I have news for him."

"I have more news than I can cope with at the moment. It's the middle of the night. Come again in the morning."

"I'll be damned if I will."

Poppy and I looked at each other. "Go away," she piped through the keyhole.

"Why *now*?" I begged.

"Because the Godforsaken aircraft to this Godforsaken place was grounded in Bombay for nine hours."

"Bombay," whispered Poppy.

"And who on earth are you?" I shouted.

"Bernard Perkins. I've been freezing here for thirty minutes. I *must* come *in now*."

Hell's fangs. Where on earth was that letter?

Wafting down the stairs, a sleazy gold satin robe drifting behind him, came Copper. "What's going on?" he yawned.

I opened the door; a tall man in a black hat rushed past me. "Where is it?"

Poppy pointed down the passage. "That way," she said.

"Who's he?" said Copper.

"And where on earth have you been?" I snarled.

"You know bloody well."

"You said . . . You . . . said . . . you told me . . ."

"Yeah, yeah, but . . ." He picked up his daughter. "What's going on, sweetheart?"

"Someone's come," said Poppy.

"Who?"

"Bernard Perkins. He said."

"Ah," said Copper.

"May I introduce myself?" I said, putting out a hand to welcome the distracted-looking figure coming back up the hall. "I am Oliver Perkins, this is my son Copland Perkins, and this is Poppy Perkins. You, I understand, are Bernard Perkins?"

"Yes."

"Yes. Shall we sit down? Let's go into the sitting room."

More lights, a heater, more proffered hands. Poppy after a moment's confusion took Bernard's then gave it back to him. Copper, not before time, tied the gaudy robe around his waist before making contact.

We sat looking at each other in the chilly room. If Poppy sat on Copper's knee all might not be well. Bernard, all arms and legs, removed his Neville Chamberlain hat. He seemed uncertain as to where to put it. If he couldn't risk the floor I was not going to help him.

"Well," I said, "welcome to Thorndon, Bernard. It is a pleasure to meet you. Yes, indeed. And how can we help you?"

Nine hours in Bombay airport had not improved Bernard, or maybe he always looked like that.

"Didn't you get my letter?"

"Yes, yes, certainly I did. It's just that I've mislaid it at the moment. Well, not mislaid. It must be at my rooms."

169

Bernard's face was green, the grey-green sludge of exhaustion. "But you must have read it."

"No, no, I can't say I have, not entirely. There must have been some emergency at the practice. Ah yes, I remember now. Bad reaction to a local — anaesthetic, I mean. Yes. And of course it's our busy time of the year, winter. You'd be amazed the number of people who want their teeth in top shape well before Christmas — it's our long holiday period of course. Sun, sea . . . barbecues require strong teeth."

"But I said I was coming!"

"Yes, yes, I do remember that and I was delighted to hear it, but I don't recall any date."

"The date is today," said Bernard, grabbing an airline ticket from his wallet and flapping it at my face. "Friday 5 June 2001. See. And I rang from the airport on my mobile but there was no answer."

"Oh," I said.

"I suppose we were all asleep," offered Poppy.

"Off you go to bed, honey," said Copper,

"But I was the one who *heard* him."

"Quick stick. Off you go."

Poppy inched her way along the sofa towards me. "Soon," she said.

"The arrangement was that I should arrive for my visit to you today. I received no notice from you to the contrary."

"Visit," I said.

"Visit," agreed Bernard. He was rising in my estimation. This grey-green-faced heap was a sticker.

"Where will he sleep?" said Poppy.

170

I gave a hesitant laugh, not nervous, it was my home after all, but I could see her point. "That is rather a problem."

"Not at all," said Copper, all bright eyed and hairy legged in his inadequate dressing gown. He patted the old sofa on which he sat. "I'll bunk down here. Delighted."

"No," I said.

"Copper," cried Teresa from the stairs. "What's going on, honey?"

Copper leapt to his feet and Poppy followed him.

"Poppy," I cried. She turned at the urgency in my voice. "Yes?"

"Would you be kind enough to sleep in Granny's and my bed tonight so Dad's cousin can have your bed."

"Will you be there?"

"Yes."

"OK, I'll go on Granny's side."

Belatedly, apologetically, I attempted the welcome the man had presumably expected.

But what on earth did he want? And where in the name of all that's merciful was that festering letter.

I offered him things. Tea? A drink perhaps? I would of course change Poppy's sheets, give him a towel. I didn't think he'd need a hot water bottle but if so . . .

His eyes were slits in the mud, drowning in sleep. "Bed," he said, "just a bed. Don't change."

"And we'll discuss things in the morning?"

"Discuss? Oh yes, yes." He groped his way to the stairway. "Yes," he said, nearly colliding with Copper who was now running down the stairs in jeans and jacket.

"See you in the morning, Bernard," he called.

Bernard crawled upwards in silence.

"Copper, *what* are you doing now?"

"Because otherwise we're in the donger, Dad, can't you see? Give me the surgery keys and I'll get the letter so we can at least know what's going before we meet up with Bernie at breakfast."

"I don't know where it is."

"Hell, well you'd better come too. You must have some sort of a clue."

Copper the proactive, the lithe lover, the gripper of crises was right. "I can't go like this," I said.

"Take the trenchcoat from the cloakroom."

"I'm not going until I know if Poppy's asleep. She's behaved impeccably. I'm not going to have her upset."

Copper sucked his teeth, bounded up the stairs to check and rattled down again holding a pair of trousers. "Here," he said, offering them to me. "She's out like a light."

And thus it was that we drove to the surgery at O four double O. It was raining. And cold.

All was far from well in my mind. If ever there was a wild goose chase this was it. I had mentioned the surgery only because it was at one remove from 59 Tinakori Road. What on earth was I going to do? And then I had a thought, a memory so crystal clear it glistened. As soon as we arrived I headed for the cupboard where the clean laundry is stowed and began to sort through the piles, restacking them neatly as I did so. Copper, after one bemused glance, went into the surgery proper. Heart thudding and head lightening, I continued my search. Halfway down the second pile of hand towels on the right-hand side I found the long thick envelope addressed to me. The last time I had seen it it had been in the bottom of the little suitcase which contained the clean laundry for the surgery. I suppose I had put it there at home in the spurious hope that I might read it at the rooms, and then forgotten all about it.

How or why Teresa had left it there, or how it had eluded Miss de Lillo's eyes I don't know. Relief flooded. A given. Definitely a given, this one. On your knees, Perkins.

It is always a pleasure to find something by using one's wits. In fact it is always a pleasure to find anything, particularly as the years advance and things begin to fly from the hand. Nevertheless this find was the full enchilada, the Daddy of them all.

I drifted the envelope before Copper's eyes, and he was courteous enough to be impressed.

"Just a hunch," I said, "just a hunch. Shall we read it now?

"Good heavens no, let's get home."

"Copper?"

"Yes?"

"I want you to know how delighted I am — about Teresa, I mean. I think you will be very happy. Both of you."

He flung his arms around me in the pallid light of the reception area and hugged. "Thanks, Olly. Thanks a lot."

"You read it first?" he said in the car.

"Won't Poppy wake up?"

"Never."

He parked his car. We walked up the path beneath the dripping pohutukawas in silence. Mine was the solemn silence of relief. The guilty pleasure of having got away with something warmed the cockles of my heart.

I opened the door. "Thank you, Copper," I said.

He grinned. "Not at all. Let's go to bed."

Poppy lay curled in the foetal position beside me, taking up less than a yard of Hester's bed length. The fleeting relief of finding the lost letter with such apparent brilliance — and in front of Copper — faded. Now I would have to do something, deal with it.

This sort of thing is usually Hester's part of ship, as indeed would have been the maintaining of Poppy's innocence. Hester has coped with things of this nature for as long as I can remember. She has perhaps spoilt me. In which case a sense of inadequacy in unexpected situations is not entirely my fault. Yes? No. Too Jesuitical by half. And, in some way these new responsibilities have given me . . . well, let's say something like a sense of ardour, mettle; have made me feel more like an effective man for all seasons rather than an elderly grass-widower dentist with cashflow problems.

Nevertheless I could see no good coming from Uncle Lionel's great-nephew's visit to Thorndon. Poppy made a wriggle as I opened the envelope, then lay still.

The first year of the new millennium, I gathered, had been as good as usual for Bernard Gurth Perkins. He introduced himself and gave me his credentials.

He was the only child of Edmund Perkins, who was the only son of my Uncle Gurth Perkins, and thus a great-nephew of the late Egbert, Lionel, my father Charles Octavius, Decima and other sisters.

He had obtained my address from the Family Bible in which Great Aunt Decima, who died in 1978 aged ninety-eight and in full possession of her faculties, had kept a record of the few remaining members of Henry Horatio Perkins' family. He, Bernard Gurth, was now the owner of the said Bible, and he had been interested to discover how, considering that Horatio and Blanche Perkins had had ten offspring, they had left very few male, or indeed female, descendants.

The letter continued:

You may be interested to hear that this letter concerns your Uncle Lionel, who having left the church not long after your father, took passage to Barbados in the 1880s.

The days of the immensely rich Planter's class and their armies of benighted bondsmen had gone. However, indentured labour was cheap, and sugar was still the most alluring crop, though it remained the hardest to get into. Lionel ploughed every penny back into the small broken-down plantation he had been able to lease, which he worked with only two chartered labourers. He bought land, employed more men, bought more land and became in time a wealthy man.

(Did he indeed? Well, well. Hear that, Father?)

I have read some of his letters (continued Bernard) and they are frankly alarming; the hours he worked, the heat, the large and sometimes contentious workforce, nothing would stop his determination to accumulate a large sum of money. All of which he later bequeathed to his youngest sister, Decima Mary, when he died in 1924. In his will he stated that Decima was precious to him not only because she was the only sibling who had ever shown him any affection whatsoever as a child, but also because she was the only one who had corresponded with him after his parents died.

(Presumably this was at the stage when Lionel was still being regarded by the rest of his family as having turned out a bit of a disappointment.)

Great Aunt Decima told me before she died that she had been thrown into confusion by this information. Her instinct had been to divide her legacy between the remaining members of Horatio's offspring; however, Egbert, an Army padre, had been killed in the War; Gurth's only son Edmund had no children at this time; and your Father, Charles, was as yet unmarried. She made no mention of her five sisters, presumably because they were married and therefore, in Decima's view, were technically no longer Perkins.

Decima, however, was concerned at the lack of twentieth-century Essex Perkins and decided to invest her considerable sum in gilt-edged securities until she died, in the hope that some more offspring would appear in the interim. Apart from a generous amount she had given to the Parish of Copland soon after Lionel's death, the two sole heirs are therefore myself and your son, Copland.

I rocked back with such astonished force that my skull cracked against the bedhead. Good God. Such things do not happen to Copland. If I'd had a hat I would have thrown it high.

So Lionel died of disappointment in the West Indies. Did he, by Jove.

And still Poppy slept and I read on.

A coda to the will dated 5 May 1955 added that Great Aunt Decima, in gratitude for her brother Gurth's generosity and his unending kindness towards her, bequeathed to his infant grandson, Bernard Gurth Perkins, the Family Bible, plus her mother's card case and father's claret jug.

Bernard's letter waffled on. How grateful he was to Great Aunt Decima, how he intended to use some of her legacy to travel the world, how he would like to make contact with the only other legatee, Copland Gurth Perkins.

Only other legatee Copland Gurth Perkins. Good God.

The letter continued:

On a more personal note. I spend a disproportionate time in the air and this year has been no exception. This year I have been summoned to Bahrain, Hong Kong, California, Connecticut, and as ever, one or two of the more wealthy parts of Europe. Wherever the rich are, Perkins is likely to turn up. Fortunately I have no objection to flying. Nor, I may say, to millionaires. It's not too bad in Business Class and in my opinion the rich have been much maligned. They are different undoubtedly, but their houses are often interesting and they themselves not necessarily niggardly.

Naturally my clients pay my fare. Whether you want the best in Indoor Swimming Pools, Conservatory Design, or a total Indoor Health Complex, you must engage the offices of our international firm, Butterworth Impact: Design for the Discerning. I am one of the design management team, combining as I do architectural training and design training skills. You may ask why does an overqualified person at managerial level spend so much time travelling. The answer is supervision, supervision, supervision. Our clients pay for perfection and it is my task to ensure they get it.

Anthea and I have separated, but I am pleased to say that we are now on friendly terms once more, albeit at a distance.

But enough of myself.

With best wishes,

Yours,

Bernard G. Perkins

The following was handwritten on another sheet of paper with a later date.

Dear Oliver,

Amazing bit of luck. Couldn't be better timed. For the first time I have been called to New Zealand. A commission in Auckland and a nibble from a place called Queenstown. The seriously rich seem to be rather thin on the ground in your country, but then your population is small.

On another note — you will, I hope, have or will shortly receive the letter from Great Aunt Decima's solicitor, J. P. Troutbeck, Colchester. As I have no address for Copland it would make sense if you told him the news yourself. I have told the firm not to send you a copy of the will until I have verified his present address. Also would you be kind enough to drop a line, or better e-mail (see above) with any news which should be added to the Family Bible. Aunt Decima stopped short at Copland. Has he any issue?

Finally may I be presumptive enough to invite myself to stay with you and your wife for a few days, from Friday to Monday perhaps (Friday 15th June to Monday 18th). We will have much to discuss and I look forward to meeting you and your family.

If I do not hear from you I shall assume this will suit.

Yours aye,
Bernard

I lay back on my pillows, my heart soaring at the beauty of it all, the breath of Copland's issue whistling gently at my ear. There is no sweeter delight for a parent than to see his child delighted. Well done, Copper. This is what our dearly loved son has needed for years. A legacy, a whopping great legacy. How thrilled Hester will be. But why doesn't the man say how much? I turned to leap out of bed in my excitement, my rush to tell him, then realised he could be — well, he could be anywhere. Copper, Copper, Copper. It was all I could do not to wake Poppy in my euphoria. As to cousin Bernard himself. A bearer of good news should never be disparaged, but his "seriously rich" comment had rankled slightly.

One would be prepared to admit one is not seriously rich oneself — in fact it would be idiotic not to — but to have one's country's paucity of the species in question aired in this way is not only insulting but incorrect. I won't stoop to naming them, in fact I wouldn't know them if I fell on them, but they exist. Many of them. Almost a glut. Mainly in Auckland, I agree, but spoors can be found elsewhere.

And this smear from the great-nephew of brother Lionel whom my father had disliked. Imagine the *Yes Sir*, and *No Sir* and *Please Sir* and *Oh Sir* of the discussion.

Bernard: "Any seriously rich in New Zealand, do you know, Sir?"
Seriously Rich: "Seriously, you mean, Bernard?"
Bernard: "Well yes, seriously, if you don't mind."
Seriously Rich: "Oh, I don't give a toss."
Bernard: "Well no Sir, I don't suppose you do."
Seriously Rich: "We have one or two trillionaires coming up the straight in my own country, as it happens."
Bernard: "Goodness me, what does that mean in round terms, Sir?"
Seriously Rich: "I don't know about round terms but the benchmarks are pretty clear."
Bernard: "Yes I suppose they would be. As to New Zealand, Sir?"
Seriously Rich: "What about it?"
Bernard: "Are there any seriously rich there?"
Seriously Rich: "Not to my knowledge."
Bernard: "Oh."

Damn cheek.
I snuggled, positively snuggled down beside Poppy.

★ ★ ★

In that drift of time between sleep and awakening I knew something good had happened. I lay with eyes closed, letting the thought seep through. Money. Copper. Good. Definitely money. I sat up. No Poppy in sight.

"Dad," called Copper from the door. He appeared in that flimsy yellow thing and handed me a mug of tea. "Tea," he said.

"How very kind, thank you."

"What does it say?"

I handed it to him. "Read it. Here. Get into Mum's side."

So there we lay, like birds in the wilderness, birds in the wilderness, birds in the wilderness. But close, very close.

Eventually he turned with the stunned grin appropriate for one surfacing from beneath a shower of gold. "Christ," he said.

"Yes, I agree."

"Why doesn't the guy say how much?"

"Exactly."

"That's the first thing, wouldn't you think?"

"Yes, I would."

He lay silent. A quick sideways glance confirmed that he was concerned: his face was frowning beneath his mess of curls; he plucked the coverlet. I had never seen that before, except in old movie deathbeds.

"You're sure there were no slaves then?"

"Quite sure. Now look Copper . . ."

He swung towards me. "It's not a question of 'Look Copper'. Indentured labour has always led to problems."

"I agree." I lay back, sipped my tea. "There are two things you can do. First, accept the money, have a look at it, roll it around the tongue a bit and hand it straight on to Amnesty. There are still plenty of horrors in the world."

"Yes," said Copper. "I could do that."

"And secondly find out how much money the legacy is."

He has a beautiful grin as well, Copper. "Yeah. And there's Poppy too, isn't there? And Teresa."

I was beginning to feel I'd had enough. "There is indeed. And Corinne and Marty and the little kids. Now if you'll excuse me I'll have a shave."

"Yeah. Bit of a wanker, old Bernard, wouldn't you say."

"Give the man a chance."

Poppy appeared, clapped her hand to her mouth to stifle mirth. "You two look like those funny men in bed on telly, and Teresa says she could do with a hand Dad."

Clutching yellow satin, Copper jumped out of bed. "You'd better get dressed too, matey. Come on."

"I can't, the man in the hat's still in there."

"Creep in, dopey, and get your gear."

"You creep with me."

"When will we ring Hester?" I said, heading for the bathroom.

"I haven't told Teresa yet. Let's make it tonight. And Dad?"

"Yes?" I said, lathering away.

"I don't get it."

"Get what?"

"Decima died in 1978."

"Yes."

"Where's the cash been up till now?"

We stared at each other.

"Good God."

"Yes," said Copper. "Come on, rabbit." He stopped, put his head around the door.

"And thanks, Dad."

"Not at all."

Teresa was pleased at the news but calm. "It will be most useful," she said as Poppy's back was turned, "but we must not talk in front of the small until Copper knows more from the tired man." She lowered her voice to a whisper. "Perhaps, I may be given a ring, a little one, small as an egg. Why not?"

The ripples of delight widened. "Olly," shrieked Poppy, waving her spoon, "I'm going to be a bridesmaid for Teresa and Dad!" Smiles all round. The other news was apparently still embargoed.

"What time d'you think he'll wake up?" said Copper.

"*Dios mio*," said Teresa, buttering toast. "How can we know?"

"I'll bet he gets jet lag," said Copper, "they all do."

"Come along, *munequita*, here are your disgusting bubbles. You were most clever last night, were you not?"

184

"You weren't in your room, Dad," explained Poppy, "so I had to get Olly."

"Mr Perkins was clever instead," said Teresa. "And here is your lunch, no raisins. We are out of raisins. Copper, did you hear? Raisins."

"OK . . . Dad?"

"Yes?

"I've still no idea, have you? If he ever surfaces we can ask him about the delay. Not that I'm worried."

"Of course not."

A quiet day, almost a dull day at the rooms. I don't remember ever being bored there before. Life seems to be abandoning reality. The drama of home life has taken over.

I wish Hester had seen me wielding the poker while Copper, presumably, lay upstairs in post-coital bliss. Everything I suspected might happen if Teresa stayed in the house has come to pass, and I am unconcerned. Nor do I blame Teresa, not for a moment. As I have mentioned before, it takes two to tango and Copper has been lacing his boots from day one. Indelicacies, not to say fornication, have occurred, innocence has been impugned but not damaged, and our disparate crew seems to be pulling well together. Added to which Bernard's news, dramatic, reeking of money and out of the blue, seems to have topped off the family merriment very nicely.

Copper is a fine young man, a bit casual in some ways but sound at bottom, and Teresa seems to me to be bonny and blithe and good as gold, an excellent

combination in anyone marrying Copland. Nevertheless I hope and trust she will give up her night job.

And now for home and the man in the hat. He can't
still be asleep.

CHAPTER
ELEVEN

In Balclutha there was a right way and a wrong way for all things, including hanging out the washing. My mother approved of this. She was, as she said, particular. She liked a tidy line. Sheets billowed first, then towels lined straight, shirts stretched tight by their tails, and socks in pairs; there must be no sagging, no sloppiness to offend the eye. If it rained they were rehung in Snow's workshop, equally tidy, equally segregated and equally taut.

She would not have approved of Mrs Mendez's clothes-drying arrangements: the crucified shirts hanging slack from their wrists, the hotchpotch of pillow and pants, the poles.

Mrs Mendez has no wish for tidiness. She already has cleanliness and godliness which should be enough for anyone, but what I notice most is how much she enjoys her days. She is a proud woman and will not let me pay board, therefore I give the money to José who will wheedle her into accepting it from him when we leave. She is devout and full of secular superstitions and the religious certainties which govern her life. She rules her family with vigour and loves everyone, including me. She has the gift of cheerfulness.

I was folding the shirt which I have been permitted to iron in the early morning before the worst of the heat began when I heard her calling, "Éster, Éster come quick. It is your man speaking. The son."

I snatched the telephone from her outstretched hand. "Copper, how lovely to hear you."

"I thought you might like to hear the news," he cried. "Teresa and I are getting married. Yeah, yeah hang on a minute . . . Poppy wants a word. I'll put her on."

Poppy tells me she's going to be a bridesmaid, Teresa tells me she is so happy and so lucky and she hopes I am happy also, and I am, I think, but it is too quick, too far away and they hardly know each other, although I don't say that, how could I.

"And Olly, let me talk to Olly." And there he is, my Oliver Gurth, calm as a still Sunday and sounding so near I could weep.

"Olly. Isn't it, isn't it . . .?"

"Wonderful," he said. "Yes it's wonderful news. Poppy thinks so, don't you. Yes, yes she does. And she's going to be . . ."

I am sniffing by now. "I know, I know, oh Olly, do you really . . . you know?"

"Of course I do. I've just said so."

"José and Juan are staying on longer. The gay and lesbian pride march is near the end of June and they want to celebrate together."

"Good. There's something else. Bernard Perkins is here."

"Who?"

"Let's try it another way. Copper has been left a lot of money."

"What?"

"Money, dosh, boodle. Stuff with the Queen on."

"Why? I mean how?"

"It's been bequeathed to him by his Great Aunt Decima Mary."

"She died years ago."

"Well yes, it's all a bit complicated as a matter of fact, but don't worry."

"I'm not worried, I'm stunned. Who told you?"

"His cousin from Britain. Bernard, the one I mentioned."

"Where's he staying?"

"At 59 with us."

"There's not enough beds."

"Yes, well . . . we're Boxing and Coxing a bit at the moment, but everything's under control. 'Steer where the masts are thickest,' that sort of thing."

"I must get home."

"That would be delightful but please, don't worry, not on our account or Bernard's. All things considered we've got a pretty taut-run ship here, haven't we, Poppy?"

"Yep."

"Hullo darling. Why's Olly gone all 'Captain Pugwash'?"

"He's the boss of us. Are you having a cool time, Granny?"

★   ★   ★

Bernard, shaved, sleek and presumably in his right mind, welcomed me into the sitting room. He looked better than when I saw him last, but not much. Teresa and Copper had gone to look for rings, he told me, and he and Poppy were playing Monopoly and he was winning.

So the lovers had taken a sicky, had they? I realise they have something to celebrate, but I disapproved on principle. Whatever that means.

"Have you, ah, discussed things with Copper?"

"Not in depth. He thought you might like to be there. Poppy and I have been arranging the chairs in the dining room — glasses, carafe of water, etc. She says that's how men have Talks on TV. Didn't we, Poppy?"

"Mm. It's your turn now, Bernard," she said.

Damned civil of Copper, considering he wouldn't be in any shape or form to discuss anything if it were not for Hester and me, I, me. Nevertheless, I was glad he had the grace to make the suggestion. Things were looking up.

Teresa had decided that we should eat in the dining room, presumably in honour of the messenger. Afterwards we could have our discussion with Bernard while she and Poppy tidied up and she would bring in the coffee and have we any port perhaps?

Port. What a good idea. I was on my knees at the bottom cupboard in an instant. No, we haven't.

The ladies left the table in due course and the three of us remained feeling slightly silly, or perhaps that was

190

only me, being the only one left in the room with no financial interest in the proceedings.

Copper led from the left. "The thing we want to know first, Bernard, is . . ."

"How much is the amount of the legacy liable to be?" said Bernard.

"Yes. And my second query is why, if Great Aunt Decima died in 1978, have we not even heard of this legacy until 2001?"

"Yes," said Bernard. "Poppy won't come in, will she? No. Good." He leaned back. The teller of tales, the one who knew, took a sip water. "It is a very sad story," he said finally.

"Yes?" said Copper.

"As you both know, Decima Perkins never married. When her brother Lionel died in 1924 she was living quietly in the village of Copland with her ageing parents. Her father had retired from his clerical duties — or as much as a clergyman can ever be said to retire. He would fill in for the current incumbent when the man in question went on holiday, and offer his assistance at busy times in the church calendar such as Christmas and Easter, when things tend to get a bit hectic.

"Henry Horatio no longer lived in the Rectory of course, but he and Blanche and Decima had bedded down in a small thatched cottage owned by the church in the village. The rent, apparently, was peppercorn. Decima told me that Henry used to say in jest that he would like to change the name from *Crumplecot* to *Almost Anything Else*. Neither he nor Blanche made

191

old bones. Henry was knocked over by a drunk on a motorcycle outside The Honest Lawyer and died aged sixty-six. Blanche followed him almost immediately. Pneumonia."

"Oh, dear," I said.

Copper sat in baffled silence.

"Yes, they both died before Lionel," continued Bernard. "I never knew the details but I did gather that there was a sort of rift between Lionel and the rest of the family. Except for Decima."

"But why was it so long . . .?" said Copper.

"A moment, just a moment. Any money Henry Horatio and Blanche had they left to Decima so she was able to continue renting *Crumplecot*. However, she was so saddened by the loss of both her parents over such a short period that she went into some sort of — well, decline, I suppose one could say. The local doctor summoned her brother Gurth Perkins from his parish in Yorkshire. The long and short of things was that he and his wife, Pauline, invited Decima to stay with them until she recovered her health and strength. She returned to *Crumplecot* about six months later, and lived there, as we know, until she died in 1978."

"That's exactly what we want to know, Bernard," said Copper. "Why the twenty-year gap?"

"Twenty-three as a matter of fact, but bear with me please."

Copper has never been good at bearing with anything, much less people.

"The secret," continued Bernard, "lies with Decima."

192

"Come off it, Bernard," said Copper. "That's pretty obvious."

"In what way?"

"May I hazard a guess?" I said.

"Certainly."

"Decima," I said after a pause, "was pregnant."

"How the devil did you know that," said Bernard.

"Just a hunch."

"What the hell's got into you, Dad? Hunches all over the place. What do you mean?"

I didn't mention the cut and thrust of lateral thinking on a mind honed by years of unravelling hidden clues, of concentrated attention to the information given. It would have sounded like boasting. Nevertheless I was pleased with myself. So pleased I could have hopped on one leg round the table.

"She'd be too old," said Copper.

"Forty-six, by my reckoning. Certainly not so usual for a *prima gravida* these days, but by no means unheard of."

Bernard's head moved slowly from side to side. "But how did you guess?"

"Two things. The fact that Decima expressed her everlasting gratitude to your grandfather Gurth and grandmother Pauline in her will, and the fact that she spent six months with them in Yorkshire, which is some considerable distance from the village of Copland."

"Why would she not go to them," said Copper, "if she was in a decline or whatever? Only place she could go, except to her sisters. Why didn't she go to a sister?"

"We can't know," said Bernard, "except for the fact that they all lived near Copland."

"So my hunch is correct?" I said demurely.

He nodded. A solemn, well-considered nod. "Yes."

"Who was the father?" asked Copper.

Bernard looked more solemn. "We shall never know."

My mind leapt to curates — not an attractive thought and one not to be voiced, but interesting nevertheless.

"Decima was a devout woman, was she not," I asked.

"She was indeed."

"Tragic. Tragic."

Copper, normally a determined champion of the rights of women, stayed on his own scent. "But we still don't know why we didn't know till now. About the legacy, I mean."

"As I told you," said Bernard, "it's a sad story."

I couldn't resist. "Was the baby handicapped in some way?" I murmured.

Bernard looked peeved. "May I ask how you leap to yet another correct conclusion?"

"Decima's age. At forty-six the likelihood of a damaged foetus is much higher."

"Any more coffee?" called Teresa from the doorway.

We thanked but declined, our minds with Decima and her lonely miseries.

Bernard broke the silence. "The baby girl was born severely handicapped both physically and mentally. Decima had been determined to take the child back to *Crumplecot*, but this proved impossible. The only place

194

she could find for the child was a grim fortress-like institution near York. Did you say something, Oliver?"

"No, no."

"It was a horrible place. The authorities advised Decima not to visit the child. She refused, and travelled to her brother's vicarage to be with her daughter whenever possible. The baby was christened Mary Pauline Gurth Perkins by her uncle Gurth."

There was nothing to say.

"Yes," said Bernard, "Lionel died the following year and Decima inherited his money. She had always known there was a private asylum with a high standard of care for the severely disabled near Copland. Their fees were commensurable with the care given, but Decima wasted no time after she heard of the legacy. She took advice from Mr Troutbeck, her solicitor in Colchester, who recommended a financial adviser — Kooble, his name was — and he knew his stuff. You and I, Copland, owe Mr Kooble our thanks, and of course Mr Troutbeck who kept a sharp eye on things."

"Yes," said Copper, looking blanker than ever.

"Mary was escorted down from Yorkshire as soon as possible and installed in Willeston House, whereupon Decima bought a Baby Austin and learned to drive it. She told me the day she passed her driving licence was one of the happiest of her life. The car gave her independence, and how else could she have seen her child. She visited Mary regularly until the day before she, Decima, died in 1978."

Bernard paused, gave a slight cough.

"Mary Perkins," he said, "died earlier this year aged seventy-five."

I put my shaking hands beneath the table and hung on tight as I thought of Decima who I gave up sending messages to years ago and the life of Mary which brought tears to the heart.

"What about a whisky, Dad," said Copper.

"No thanks."

"Bernard?"

"Thank you. No ice."

Copper put a hand on my shoulder and squeezed. "I'll get you one anyway, Dad."

I turned to Bernard. "How do you know all this detail?"

"Decima told me most of it. She was a wonderful woman. I knew her quite well, but she never breathed a word about the legacy, or Mary. I didn't know that until Troutbeck read me the will."

"Did she leave her brother Gurth any money?"

"No. She wanted to, but neither he nor Pauline would accept it."

"Why not? What in heaven's name did Uncle Lionel do?"

"I've no idea. No one never mentioned it."

"Hmm. Extraordinary. Quite extraordinary."

Copper arrived with whiskies. I took mine, lifted it high then lowered it. I had thought of making a toast to Decima but refrained. Wouldn't do, wouldn't do at all. However much she deserved our thanks, it seemed crass not to include Mary. We sat solemn as judges eyeing other judges, nodded occasionally. I had to get out. Quickly.

"If you'll excuse me, I'll leave you two to it. Find the girls."

"Hang on a minute, Dad," said Copper. "If Mary lived till she was seventy-five, Bernard, why was there any money . . . well, you know, left."

Bernard chuckled, an odd sound at the best times. "Oh, no, no, no. That was just the yearly interest on the investments which enabled Mary to be moved to Essex. Decima never touched the capital except for her car and a large donation or two to the parish, that sort of thing."

"Oh," said Copper. He dragged a hand through his hair, stared at it. "In that case, it, the capital I mean, must be . . ."

Bernard was filled with remorse. "I do apologise. Of course you want to know the amount of your legacy. Of course you do . . . I should have told you. How remiss. The first thing you'd want to know, and here I am knowing all the time and not coming to the point."

"How much is it?" said Copper.

"Excuse me," I said, and strode out whisky in hand.

I was at a loose end and felt like one. Delighted for Copper but extraneous, irrelevant, dispirited. Where were my girls?

They were sitting at the kitchen table talking, Teresa with coffee and Poppy with a fluffy hot chocolate drink.

I picked up the packet, gave it a casual glance as a way of indicating that I was now present, was rewarded with a grin from Poppy and a wide smile from Teresa.

The fluffy drink made no claim as to health, wealth or happiness, or any other benefits for the purchaser. It was fun, undiluted frothy fluffy fun. The hot drink of choice in Room 4B required nothing more. Horlicks, the bedtime drink of my youth, had claimed to prevent Night Starvation, for heaven's sake: "Quick, the Horlicks."

Similarly, the advertisement for the contemporary Peppy's Indigestion Cure had showed a photograph of a white carpet with a black hole in it. The caption beneath was alarming. *The acid in your stomach could burn a hole in the carpet.* I remember asking Charles Octavius how the acid got out of the stomach. He replied the picture was not to be taken literally. It was more in the nature of a metaphor.

We scared more easily then.

I put down the packet.

"He'll wear all his stuff, won't he?" said Poppy.

"Oh no, honey. He couldn't be MC in his Fireman gear."

"Why not?"

Teresa explained that a wedding is more formal. "The last thing you'd want would be a Fireman for MC. His helmet for example."

"I think his helmet would add tone," I said.

Teresa was not convinced. The priest might not like it and then where would they be. The priest would like the flamenco, said Poppy. She and Ruby and the other kids were practising like mad. She stopped, put a finger to her mouth at the thought — she would have to change, wouldn't she, she didn't want to muck up her bridesmaid frock.

They moved on to sequins.

I drifted away to be greeted by Copper in the hall. "Olly, he said, "I was looking for you. Come and have a talk."

"We've just had one. Where's Bernard?"

"He's gone to bed. Jet lag. He said to say goodnight to you."

"Thank you."

"I'd better tell Teresa about the . . . about the cash."

"She's in the kitchen with Poppy."

"Oh, well, I'll just say hello."

I recalled the constant need to be near, to see, to touch, to sit beside; the knot in the stomach when some oaf claimed closer proximity to one's love. The time when Hester was posted to the station in the Main Hall where Talbot operated. The image of his leer remained for years, sharp as the flash of a jumping fish.

"Let's leave it till the morning," I said. "I've a bit of a headache for some reason."

"There won't be time then. I've got things to say."

"Tomorrow evening then," I said, heading for the stairs.

"You'll be tucked up before Poppy."

I had forgotten that. Blast. "Is there anything wrong with that?"

He grinned. "Not a thing."

Miss de Lillo also wanted to talk. Once again we went through our little song and dance act as to who sits

199

where in the surgery. This time I insisted on my having the Planmeca Prostyle. As I had suspected, it is uncomfortable unless one is laid out flat.

"John arrived last week," she said.

"Goodness me. I had no idea. Would you like some time off?"

She gave an involuntary frisson, declined the offer and told me she had had a terrible weekend. Terrible. John had arrived on Thursday.

Thursday, which was Thursday? Thursday was last week in that other world before the wheels fell off and Copper hit wealth. The day after Wednesday when Amber Priddle blew the gaffe on Poppy's Morning Talk and cousin Bernard arrived.

"Thursday," I said.

"Right from the start it was awful."

"Perhaps you'd rather not tell me."

No, no, she wanted to. She told me what a shock it was, the first sight when he came out from Customs. How she could hardly recognise him, bald as a coot, well why not, it was years since he and Lilian had made their trip here. And she had forgotten what a boomer he was. Not just a loud voice but *booming*. And he'd put on weight — gained, he called it — well she didn't mind that either, she knew she'd put on a kilo or two, we all do don't we, or else it's nothing but skin and bone, and anyhow she'd never been one to judge by appearances. No, it was none of that really, it was this weird feeling, really weird, that all she wanted in the whole world was for John to turn round and go straight back through Customs or wherever and never come out again.

And to think how shattered she'd been all those years ago when she'd had his Dear John letter. It had been just like the one in the song, how he had hated to write, how he knew how heartbroken she'd be etc., etc. She had to laugh now, but it was no joke at the time. Damn cheek if I'd excuse her French.

And now, well now she knew, was more sure than she'd ever been in her whole life, that his coming again had been a dreadful, dreadful mistake.

Why was she telling me all this? People keep doing it, and now Miss de Lillo. Me of all people.

I nodded.

And it got worse, she continued. She felt sick right from the first moment she saw him all so cheerful and booming and not a word about poor Lil, and after all it had been only a few months ago. She, Miss de Lillo, was being unfair again, she knew he was probably being tactful, but she was a nice girl, Lil, and they'd had a lot of fun together. It seemed a bit weird not mentioning her — or it had to Miss de Lillo anyhow.

Her face was now puckered with distress, her hands clenched. My poor friend, my stalwart friend. Oh dear.

I looked around for help. The pink self-filling Rinse Please glass was no use. "Would you like a glass of water, Eloise?"

The sound of her given name made her jump. "No thanks, I hate water. And anyway it just went on and on, looking at things all over Wellington and him bellowing away and me trying to be nice, I can't tell you what it was like, then finally thank goodness it was Sunday and I'd asked him around for my fish pie. He said there was nothing he liked so much as home cooking and we'd have a great time just the two of us together like in days gone by — he actually said that, Mr Perkins, I mean . . ."

"Oh dear."

"Well it was, wasn't it, and things got worse. I mean I'd worried away to myself, hadn't told anyone — well nobody except you — but I had also wondered whether I'd really like San Diego. Being me, I mean. It's hard to tell isn't it, and it would certainly be different. The thing I kept thinking about was that I know I like it here, but how do I know I'd like it there as much, even if the climate's as lovely as they say."

"Quite. That's a good point. By the way, have we any patients this morning?"

"Not till 10.30. Mrs Simmonds wants her plate tightened again."

"Ah. You were saying?"

"Yes, well, what I meant was I realised that I was much more worried about being with John than I was about being in America. I couldn't stand him . . . That sounds awful but I can't tell you what it was like."

Don't let her cry. Please.

"Yes," she sighed, "after the fish pie I told him, and would you believe it he was mad as hops and so rude and furious it made things easier in a way, and now he's all packed up and he's off on a bus trip tomorrow."

I had to say something. "Where?"

"Down south. But what I really wanted to do — and I'll keep my eye on the time, don't worry — is to thank you very much indeed."

"Me?"

"Yes, it made it so much easier to decide, well, not when I saw him again, I knew it straight off that I couldn't, but before that I'd been worried ever since I'd had his letter about him coming. I love my work here, and working with you Mr Perkins is what makes it so lovely, and I couldn't bear the thought of leaving you. I mean I know it all backwards, the work, don't I, and what would you do without me, that's what I kept thinking."

Another turn of the screw. Jesu man, you keep them coming.

A better man than I would have told his devoted assistant immediately that her job was in imminent danger of disappearing. Even if the practice sold I fear the new incumbent would prefer someone a little more, how shall I say, racy. Blonde and perky, if my own dentist's nurses are anything to go by. *Perky.*

"Thank you, Miss de Lillo. I am sure you have made the right decision, but please, I beg you, never consider the practice, not for a moment. That is my concern and besides, things change so, don't they."

"Yes," said Miss de Lillo.

"Now how about a cup of coffee before Mrs Simmonds' plate?"

Miss de Lillo clasped her knobbly hands together and laughed. "NATO Standard, coming up," she said and bustled out of the surgery.

I was right, things do change. The NATO Standard joke had finally stalled. Gone with the booming John. Repetition had failed them both.

Now I would have to work out how to break the news to her, to soften the blow, to find the phrase that meant redundant. There would be plenty of time, however.

> *Time for you and time for me*
> *And time yet for a hundred indecisions.*

CHAPTER
TWELVE

It's an odd thing about pigeons. They have an impact on the urban scene far beyond their presence. They induce a range of emotions in people; some they infuriate almost beyond endurance (my barber Paddy calls them rats with wings) others accept them as a fact of city life, along with the squashed remnants of chewing gum and cigarette butts. Only a few succumb to their pompous charm.

Certainly pigeons defecate in public places and with frequency. It is in their nature to do so, as is their propensity to carry lice. But look at their beautiful globular forms, their restrained gents-suiting colour range illuminated with an occasional flash of blue which contrasts with their beady eyes and their to-hell-with-the-lot-of-you attitude to mankind. Another thing which pleases me is their lack of chat. You never see them *confer*. They just keep peck, peck, pecking, all for one and they're the one. And they know how to get home.

Yes, I would have considered myself pro pigeon on the whole.

I had stopped outside Old St Paul's on my way home, a thing I do quite often these days. You don't realise how steep the slope up Mulgrave Street is until you walk it, and Old St Paul's and its environs give me a perfect excuse to catch my breath while admiring the green grass and the grace of the pohutukawas growing wide and free as they should instead of *peeping in the windows of the house etc.* All these, plus the pleasing proportions of the original wooden cathedral, are well worth looking at.

There were a few pigeons strutting about. You don't need many. I wondered, not for the first time, why they bother to come up here. Slim pickings I would have thought, unless the busloads came prepared.

I sauntered in the Out gate and stood still. A quick glance and the pigeons took no further notice, merely continued their industrious pecking. One braver or more stupid than the rest lifted near me, shimmered in the air for a second and seemed about to land on my right shoe. Instinctively, without volition, my right leg swung back and forwards in a perfect punt.

It was near as a toucher. The pigeon, squawking with rage, lifted and circled and, still muttering to itself, landed on the grass beyond. I stood stricken with guilt, glanced around in the hopes of seeing no one. What in heaven's name had possessed me? It had pink feet too. Does that mean it was a stripling, or is that only gulls? Which would be worse: unprovoked violence against youth or age? Not good.

An Asian couple stood side by side by the picket fence, spluttering and giggling and making agitated gestures with their hands to indicate they would be delighted if they could take my photograph. I was

206

extracting myself as best I could from this contretemps, but worse was at hand. I recognised, from frequent passings and repassings up and down the street, the face of the man who stood staring beside the disappointed Asians. A man with whom I had exchanged an occasional nod and nothing more. One whom I had subconsciously dismissed as an incipient captain of industry, a man with a future, a headhunter's dream. A pill.

And yes, the lip did curl. "Taking a day off are we, St Francis?"

I ignored him and sauntered out the other gate, trying not to shake as I did so. To my surprise I found euphoria rising with every step. I, Oliver Perkins, had jolly nearly punted a pigeon, though fortunately on deconsecrated ground.

However, euphoria did not last, it's not meant to. Like bliss it is ephemeral, particularly in cases such as this; it had seeped through the soles of my feet by the time I reached home. I realised that not only had I behaved badly but presumably I would have to spend the rest of my working life avoiding dirty glances from the Friend of Sister Pigeon. Or Brother.

If Hester were home she'd have comforted me; been brisk and bracing, told me not to fuss, that the pigeon would have forgotten all about it by now, and if I thought my reflexes were better than those of an urban pigeon I could think again. She was right, of course. Birds are creatures of instinct. When punted they rise. They do not hold grudges.

There was, however, some good news at home. Bernard had announced he was going down to Queenstown to check out his nibble and would be leaving the day after tomorrow. He also put our minds at rest as regards his presence at the wedding. After Queenstown he would be heading for his good friends, Trish and Johnny Hobhouse at Potts Point, Sydney, with whom he would be tied up for some time. Useful contacts etc. as well as the social side, but he could fly back to Thorndon at a moment's notice. Send an e-mail and he'll be here.

I was glad to see that Teresa was preparing a farewell feast for him; one of massive proportions and unknown ingredients. He is an honourable man, Bernard Gurth, and has brought good news. He is welcome at any time, but not for long. He makes me feel irrelevant in my own house.

Copper appeared, accompanied by whoops of joy from the sitting room. Poppy must be beating Bernard at Snap again. "Can I have a word, Dad?"

You wouldn't read about it. You simply would not read about it. *Can I have a word, Dad?* The words must be branded on my withered rump.

"The dining room was all right last night," I said, a remark so daft it surprised us both.

I have mentioned before that I have always been an advocate for regularity and routine and I also like to know where I am, to be part of an organised system. But look where all this Routine and System had landed me. Walk to work. Work. Depressing talk with Cashem. Walk home. Talk with Copper. Friendly nods from

Poppy. Busy smiles from Teresa. Talk to Copper. Walk to work. Work — and so on ad nauseam. And if I did sell the practice, or "attempt to sell", as Cashem put it, whither Miss de Lillo? *Quo vadis* Eloise?

Oh damn and blast and bloody hell.

Charles Octavius never swore.

And look where it got him.

"What's up, Dad?" said Copper as we sat looking at each other across the table.

"Up? Nothing is up, nothing at all."

"I thought you sounded a bit down."

"When have I have ever been down? What did you want to talk to me about?"

"Don't you want to know how much I'll get?"

"Nothing to do with me."

"Yeah, but aren't you *interested* . . . "

"Not at all," I lied.

"It's a lot. Poppy'll be sitting pretty."

"Good."

"Yeah, and I'm going to make over some of it to you and Mum, and that's final."

"Don't be ridiculous."

Home truths followed. The cut and thrust and traditional tedium of Copper and my discussions continued until I was twitching.

Copper lifted his game. "Mum won't be such a dope. She'll be chuffed. Wait and see."

Nicely put. She would be too. Hester is nothing if not clear sighted.

I tried another tack. "Why do you want to do this?"

"Because you've earned it, you stupid old . . . oh never mind. It's no different from my winning Lotto, being a pop star, a celebrity chef. They're forever buying their parents houses, entertainment centres, Volvos, cruises to Alaska."

"I am not a stupid old fart."

"OK. Sorry, sorry, rude, bad. But let's be realistic. It's high time you sold that tired old practice, and don't mention the chair. Teresa's all for it and Mum will be too."

"How dare you discuss the practice with Teresa."

"I discuss everything with Teresa."

How I abominate this passion for *sharing*, this fear of being alone with your own indecisions, this need to belong. I said nothing.

"All right then," he continued, "it's not tired. Good position, great potential. I could write the ad myself. You're seventy-five years old, man. Any minute soon you'll be creeping up and down Mulgrave Street on your Zimmer frame."

"I've told you before. I can't leave Miss de Lillo in the lurch. She has decided not to marry her cousin so she can continue working for me."

Copper has never been close to Miss de Lillo. In his youth he composed crude chants around her name, Eloise being one which lends itself to rhymes like *squeeze, sneeze, bee's knees etc.*

"Don't worry about Eloise," he said, "she'll bounce back. She's probably just being nice."

Now he had managed not only to insult my good friend, who he obviously sees as some sort of offshoot

210

of the exhausted practice, but to dismiss my concern for her. To him there was no dilemma. Eloise gets the breeze.

And he is right, look at the facts. And look at his generosity. His goodwill shows in his face, his large easy face in his large easy-as-you-go frame. And not only is he right. He has an ally. As regards selling the practice, he and Cashem are as two buttocks of one bum. (Can't remember who said it, but it was Chesterton and Belloc who shared the original fundament.)

Copper put out his hand. The thought that he might be sorry for me terrified.

"Got an old envelope?" he said.

I handed him the one from Cashem's latest scorcher. Copper scribbled for a second and gave it back. I took the limp thing without enthusiasm.

> *Options re Sale of Practice*
> <u>*A*</u>*. Continue to practise.*
> *Result — a) Go bankrupt.*
> *b) Exit Eloise.*
> <u>*B*</u>*. Sell practice.*
> *Result — a) Hopefully avoid bankruptcy.*
> *b) Exit Eloise.*

I crossed out the word *Hopefully* and handed it back.

Copper shook his head. "It's a bad call, Dad. You're in a no-win situation."

"For God's sake stop talking jargon."

"Your jargon is my words. And I'm only trying to *help*."

Which can be the most choke-inducing phrase known to man.

"Thank you," I said.

The longer Hester has been away, the more I have become aware that yes, there is life after dentistry even without crosswords. That new vistas do open up but only if given a push. The thought has also occurred that I might be in danger of becoming an old curmudgeon. One who more and more enjoys less and less and tells you so.

And Copper, my auburn-haired cherub, wants to avoid this decline. He has mentioned money for aged parents. Having almost snapped off his head, I now realise this might well be a change in the right direction. Money does not bring happiness but it can help you enjoy your misery in comfort.

Us, that magic word. There will be us. *Two legs good, four legs better.* Hester will be there.

I leapt to my feet, or tried — I had been sitting for so long I had to stamp around a bit to get the knees going. I hobbled round the table and embraced the now upright Copper, who welcomed me into bear-like arms.

"Thank you Copper," I said, and kissed him.

"Good on y', Dad," he said. "You've earned it."

Over his left shoulder I saw a van labelled *Cogent Communications* drive down our neighbour's concrete path and park at the back door. Libby and Clive Wishart have solved the communication problem. Just sent for the van.

"One other thing Dad . . . What are you grinning at?"

Nothing.

"I've been thinking. Teresa and I haven't made any decision yet but we've been talking around it a lot . . ."

"Around what?"

"I haven't decided, as I said, but things seem to be shaping up to it, and like I said Teresa agrees right along the line. I've more or less decided to stay with WINZ."

God Almighty. All Snow Hope's rainy day stash blown to the winds. I could have sent Hester myself. Hester, I could have said, Hester my sweet, please take . . .

The van next door had gone. Cogent or not cogent, it had delivered the goods.

"You surprise me," I said.

Copper leaned forward. "Yeah, I see what you mean, but it's like this. We've talked it through and we agree the real trouble was that I was so fed up with myself and life in general, well you know what I was like, but now . . . Well hell I've got Teresa and Poppy, quite apart from all the cash and . . ."

To hell with reticence. "How much is it?"

"A million pounds."

The words came out with a squeak: "Between you?"

"Hell no. Each."

"Oh."

"So what with all that and quite apart from charities I think the least I can do is to give more of myself, if you see what I mean."

"No, I don't."

Copper laughed, one of those big sweaty forgiving laughs. "Teresa understands perfectly. I mean we'll have so much . . ."

"There are two points here. Forgive me for saying so, but your assumption that your absence at WINZ will make any difference to the well-being of your clients is tosh. They won't even notice whether you're there or not, why should they? And secondly, what's happened to your passion for Art History and the renaissance of New Zealand Art?"

"One difference is I'll be able to buy it."

"True, but unworthy of your altruism. And what about Teresa?"

"I'm going to buy her a cafe. She's hell bent on that, until the kids arrive anyway. We were thinking we might be interested in the surgery building if nobody wants to buy it."

Copper, Copper, Copper. But he is not a thankless child, not by any means. Look at him. He wants "to set Hester and you up". He wants to save everything and everybody, to love the whole damn world till it drops.

"Later on we'll probably get a lifestyle block. Teresa loves hands-on farming and it'll be great for the kids."

"Won't The Tulip and El Toro be competition?"

"They're only coffee and cupcakes. We'd be good — best coffee in town, Spanish food, open till late." He was warming to the theme. "Heh. Miss Eloise could be front of the house."

"Ha ha."

214

"Early shift of course. Why not? She's a people person. She'd love it."

I woke up with the tinkedly plonkety rhythm of *Happy days are here again* banging around inside my skull. It was still there as we waited for Hester at the airport.

And there she was, waving wildly as she appeared from Customs, smiling as she edged past men and women with placards who while away their lives waiting for people with impossible names. She walked into my arms.

"Hullo sweet," she said, her free hand stroking my back.

"Hullo," I said, and everyone was smiling and enfolding other people and Poppy with her hair tied up in knobs was jumping up and down like a piston chanting cool, cool, cool.

As soon as I saw Olly, and Teresa and Copper glued together with scarcely a hand spare to wave, but one of Teresa's free to clutch Poppy's while she jumped, I knew that any doubts I had about how the marriage would work, vis-à-vis Poppy's welfare, had disappeared. My feet were itching with excitement.

I also realised after about five minutes that I would not be called upon to mastermind the wedding. Teresa, unflappable and good-natured, was born to organise. No wonder her mother is proud of her. She begs for news of them all, every message from Madrid, all details, her mother's asthma, her aunt's back, her brother's new boyfriend.

There is so much to be heard. I attempt some answers in my Spanish but Teresa can scarcely understand a word.

A perfect homecoming and Olly agrees.

The house is more welcoming than I have ever seen it and I am home and there is a great deal of talk and tonight I will be in my own bed with Olly.

And then it will be the wedding.

People have told me that funerals often get a bigger turnout. Must be something to do with finality, I suppose. That now or never feeling.

I myself prefer weddings, though I have attended some ghasters in the past. Talbot's, for example, was a disaster, but Copper's and Teresa's wedding — ah that has had the makings of a good party from the beginning despite the fact that Señor and Señora Mendez decided to save their trip till the babies arrive, and Ben and Doug and the rest of the Balclutha contingent are in Argentina supporting a Southland School Rugby Tour. Four sons playing, four parents cheering, or booing "On y'bike, ref". And all of them happy.

Other people have come from miles. José and his new boyfriend Juan arrived wreathed in happiness. Corinne and Marty and the little kids flew in from the Coromandel on Copper's and Teresa's insistence and funding. I had been nervous about this. Corinne has never struck me as a merry person. Not being one myself I felt for her, but after sitting snarling at the bar with Marty for half an hour or so she mellowed somewhat. The little kids required no stimulants; two in number and virtually indistinguishable, they arrived hell-bent on having a good time. They came with a whoop and came with a call and proceeded to run around the large rooms of Harbour Lights Function Centre in circular directions, dropping periodically to slither on their stomachs and nip unwary adults' ankles. Until Poppy put a stop to it.

Bernard came winging in from Potts Point in full fig and excellent spirits.

He spent some time in expressing his sorrow to Hester at having missed her during his former stay but was able to reassure her that he had been well looked after by the shakedown team. After, he added, some tense moments through the keyhole on his arrival at 59 Tinakori Road at O three double O, ha ha.

His nibble in Queenstown had turned into a munch which was satisfactory, and as for Points Point; Trish and Johnny had turned themselves inside out on his behalf. Quite apart from which they were such a fun couple.

"Tell me, Bernard," I said, "where is Decima buried?"

"In the old churchyard at St Michael's. There were still a few plots left then."

"And Mary? We don't know any of the details."

"No. I was in Los Angeles at the time and Troutbeck took over. Cremated. In a box in the coat cupboard of his chambers at the moment. We were thinking of putting an urn on her mother's grave. That's something I must finalise with Copland before I go."

"Yes. There must be a plaque."

"Of course, of course." He drifts away towards the nearest Harbour Lights waiter. I wish him joy of Copper's wine: he deserves every drop.

I turn to find Hester, my lode-star, my communicator, at my side. I have to admit I have slipped a little in that regard now Hester is home. What is the point of attempting to keep information in the mind so that one can be up with the play, a keen hands-on father/father-in-law/grandfather who knows details of every arrangement when said arrangements have so often been unmade, remade or abandoned completely.

The priest of choice, for example, turned out a disappointment. He preferred to officiate only at weddings of first-time-rounders and in churches. Teresa didn't press him. She saw the Padre's point. Her exotic dancing colleague Ces's mother-in-law Gwendolyn was a certified marriage celebrant and would be more than happy to oblige. She hadn't operated at Harbour Lights before but she thought it would be especially nice in winter, still being pitch dark at the end of August and the lights on the water more lovely than ever. She thought it would make a spectacular venue and only one little bridesmaid would make things easier as well. I heard this from the horse's mouth when we first met Gwendolyn, but the information regarding flowers, food, drink, clothes, invitations and music, music, music had flowed past, leaving me bobbing in my cockleshell of ignorance and glad of Hester.

Tonight, the night of the wedding, she is looking her best in something floaty. She appears at my side

218

occasionally to introduce some unknown, to pat my hand and whirl away to welcome more.

After an hour or so I felt a pleasant sensation seeping through me. Is it possible that after all these years I have finally got the hang of social intercourse.

There are many people present and undoubtedly they are all determined, like the little kids, to have fun, to celebrate, to wish Teresa and Copper well and speed them on their way — and *I don't have to do anything*. Or rather all I have to do is to smile benignly and lift a glass occasionally in an All Hail sort of way and instantly young and beautiful people, many of whom look to be of Spanish persuasion, surround me and hail back. As long as you don't snarl, and I think even Corinne has stopped that by now, people seem glad to see you though you don't have the slightest idea who they are or what is going on.

Emboldened by this revelation I go in search of Poppy and find her sitting on the floor beside the percussion section of what looks like a small band; she is dispensing lurid-coloured fizzy drinks with straws to the two cross-legged little kids. I get down to her level and edge nearer.

"Poppy, do you know what's happening?"

"Don't blow, Roan. You're tragic. *Suck*, like this." She turns to me. "How d'y' mean happening?"

"Well, when do Teresa and Copper actually get married and do we sit down to eat? Things like that."

"Hang on." Poppy jumps to her feet in her shimmering iridescent tube of a bridesmaid frock, slips a hand beneath with the manual dexterity of a nubile

219

tennis star producing the second ball, and reveals a programme. "You should have one of these. Take it."

"Thank you. And Poppy, I think you look very pretty."

A nervous moment. "I don't wanna look *girly*," she says.

"No, no . . ." I'd be dashed if I'd say "cool" . . . "Ravishing," I said.

"Gross. Aw Roan, what y'done *now*?"

The programme reveals all. I am going to sit, I am going to eat, I am going to have a good time and so is everyone else. The scrum around the bar has been a sort of preliminary canter — what in my student days Talbot and Jackson would have called a Thrash. I wonder once more what has happened to them. Even if they died disappointed but stinking rich in the West Indies like Great Uncle Lionel, what had become of their loot? Nothing as tragic and Grand Guignol and unlikely as Lionel's, I'll be bound.

Hester reappears. "I've been looking everywhere for you."

Coral, that was the colour. Coral. "You look ravishing," I say.

"Really? How kind of you to say so. Have you met Juan?"

"I think so. Let's sit down."

"It's a bit early but never mind."

We have our own seats right in the front with our individual white daisies and cards telling us who we are. Even as we settle Jake the Firefighter appears. Leaping, prancing, practically turning handsprings in

220

the air comes José's friend who is to be the Master of Ceremonies at Harbour Lights on the occasion of the wedding of his good friends Teresa and Copper.

Still whirling and twirling he invites us to hang on to our seats. Bernard, who has also found his daisy at our table, grips the rim of his chair as suggested. Thinks it is an earthquake drill perhaps, or is it his training, his ability to follow instructions to the letter, his delight in giving satisfaction *now*.

Jake is a wonder to behold. What a strutter he is, this man. His golden helmet, clanking with chinstraps and chains in all directions, his jacket scorched with previous encounters, he is as light in his massive rubber boots as the trainee flamenco squad, if not more so.

"Does he get to take his gears off?" whispers Poppy who has found her daisy beside Bernard and is ready for anything.

Jake disillusions her and the rest of his audience. He is here strictly for MC duties only, he explains, and this is the only suit he's got.

Whirling a heavy-duty chain in the air with one finger he calls, "And all you ladies and gentlemen, you riff-raff at the back, won't get anywhere with those catcalls, so calm down. It's not that sort of party. Right?" He puts a hand to his ear. "Right!" roars the function centre.

"There are kids here, millions of them," he continues, "so watch where you put y'feet. Now, you all found y'table and daisy? Good. Now let's run through the programme, should be one sitting by each daisy. Got it. Good."

I am warming to Jake, he has Harbour Lights in his hands as he runs through the sequence of events. The next thing up is the *Ceremony*, which he pronounces like an American decked out in a woolly suit with golden helmet in his hand. After that we'll have the *Wedding Breakfast*, the feed.

Hand in hand from somewhere come Teresa and Copper, she wearing what I assume is a Spanish version of a chaste bridal gown plus an ancient shawl sent by her mother and delivered into safe keeping by José and Juan.

We stand for the ceremony, which does not take long. Gwendolyn, the celebrant, an exuberant lady with a lot of puffy grey hair and gold rings, is brisk and to the point. *Do you etc.? Yes, and what about you? — I pronounce you both man and wife. And now she'd just like to say one or two words to the happy couple, personally, and she'll keep the words short.* Which she does: *Honoured to be asked, knows them both well, wishes them all the luck in the world etc.*

A curiously shy little procedure, the ceremony, or so I find it, possibly because I miss the frilled priest, the billowing white sleeves, the established ritual. Though I don't remember missing any of them at our wedding.

Nor do Copper and Teresa. They gaze into each other's eyes, serene as lotus on a distant pool. The rest of us make a background but little more.

Poppy too is transfigured, shimmering and slinky and deadly serious as she stands beside José who is Best Man. Roan and the other little kids, the flamenco

222

dancers, even Jake the Firefighter have slid off the edge of her world.

I take Hester's hand. She has tears in her eyes. "Where's Corinne?" she whispers.

Was ever a moment so flattened. "Probably throwing up in the powder room."

"*What?*"

"Sssh."

And we break into applause for the happy couple and the celebrant, and the air is filled with cheerful ribaldry and laughter and congratulations and I sit down with my glass and Poppy comes and sits on my knee. Copper and Teresa and José and Juan join us and life is good.

Then we are eating good food and sipping an occasional glass, then there are photographs, after which we get into a spot of discreet carousing that is less discreet on the outer edges of the party which I seem to remember happened in student Thrashes as well. Jake the MC continues to whip things along with a drum-roll. He announces that Poppy and Ruby, Cassandra and Jade and Greta will now give a demonstration of the flamenco as taught them by the bride herself who has also supplied the flamenco guitar tape.

With lip-chewing care and heavy breathing and attention to detail, the hellers from 4B, decked out in swirling skirts and small shawls, perform their nascent flamenco, which is followed by tumultuous applause.

"Where is Poppy's bridesmaid's frock?" I whisper.

"What?"

223

"Bridesmaid's frock."

"Sssh."

The flamenco dancers sink into deep curtseys and run for cover, and Teresa is on her feet, her fingers snapping like castanets as she signals for the tape to continue and pulls José from his deep conversation with Bernard.

Ah, but that is an experience.

I feel ice on the backbone; Hester's mouth is hanging wide as the stealthy predatory movements begin and the straight-backed *aristos* circle and the music insists. Hester's hand is gripping mine and Poppy, once more a bridesmaid, is on my knee again and the tempo quickens and the heads lift and Poppy is so transfixed, so tense I fear she might wet her pants — why I don't know, little girls don't as a rule, but the intensity of the small skinny body on my knee seems about to self-destruct, to fly apart.

As do the rest of Harbour Lights. They are on their feet, the guests surging forward wanting to *see*, to absorb this grave and stirring dance. And then Copper is on the mini stage, pushing past Jake the Firefighter with one large hand to rescue his bride. And the crowd goes mad. Everyone is dancing, everyone is singing, Bernard seems to have disappeared.

"Come outside," I say to Hester.

"No, let's dance."

I have never considered myself much of a dancer and Hester agrees, but the whole thing is easier now there are no actual *steps*. A vague bobbing up and down and an occasional swing to left or right will get one through.

You don't have to get anything *right* now, and the music is much the same. A strong beat and a loud noise and you're away. Gone are the maudlin lyrics of our youth —

> *If I sent a rose to you*
> *For every time you made me blue*
> *You'd have a room full of roses —*

A good thing on the whole, though they served us at the time.

Poppy is dancing with Jake, and Juan, the most beautiful man in the world, slinks around his lover, and the little kids join up with those from 4B in their attempts to tunnel through locked thighs, or make cutting-out strikes on sweets and fizzy drinks.

There is too much to laugh about, too many to avoid on that tiny dance floor. We return to our table where Bernard is locked in conversation with Ces, Teresa's colleague. She is dressed in black, her creamy breasts presented at eye level. Bernard seems in danger of falling head first into what my mother would have described as his friend's bust.

Hester and I creep away to find a couple of empty seats and a bottle and a glass or two. We toast each other, beaming.

"Pure happiness," she says.

"I agree."

"What shall we do to keep it topped up? Where shall we go? Soon."

"In the whole world?"

"Why not, as long as it's not a cruise. We can keep cruises for when we're old."

"Yes."

"Not that I've anything against Alaska," she says, reaching for a bottle of rather nice Chardonnay.

"Bit chilly perhaps."

"I'm looking forward to Essex. Can't wait. And I like the idea of Cornwall."

"Yes."

"Look." She points at the tiny dance floor; there, before our eyes, circling decorously amidst the frenzied jiggers and bumpers and slinkers and grinders, appearing and disappearing and maintaining strict tempo, are Bernard and Miss de Lillo in her green.

"He must have had lessons," says Hester.

"Has he ever mentioned Anthea to you?"

"Never."

"Why are we whispering?"

"I don't know."

"And of course we'd go and come back via New York."

"Yes." She flings her arms around me, kisses me soundly. "We'll find the man and his *python* on Broadway."

"Of course we will."

She sighs. "Dear Copper."

"Indeed. And look at the lights."

It is black dark beyond the wide windows. Shimmering ribbons of purple, orange and pink light continue their snapping and reforming and snapping again in the inky sea around us.

226

"Physicists have names for reflections in water," I say. "Scientific names. Quite cosy they are too. Crinkles and wrinkles, something like that."

"I didn't know that."

We sit in silence. The wooden footbridge leading to Queen's Wharf is floodlit from below, transforming its mundane shape into a swathe of bright glowing colour, a numinous splendour of light.

I shiver, turn to Hester. "How would you describe that colour?"

"Blue," she says. She jumps to her feet.

Transparent coral stuff drifts across me as she bends to drop a kiss on my thinning hair.

"You're quite happy here, aren't you, Olly," she says. "I must dance with José."

And she runs.

Also available in ISIS Large Print:

Man-Made Fibre

Francine Stock

"Stock writes with cool intelligence"   **The Times**
"A major new talent"   **Mail on Sunday**

Love, marriage and ambition at a pivotal moment when the man-made world of the 1950s is about to change . . .

It's the start of the 1960s in a smart English suburb. Blonde, perfect Patsy is the ideal wife — attractive, ambitious, giving form to her husband's life, and style to their fabulous interior décor. Alan, too, has film-star good looks but it's his work that defines him. He's a scientist on the verge of a big breakthrough. His corporation is in the race to find the new wonder fibre that blends convenience with style for the modern executive, and Alan is jetted over to Head Office in Delaware. But for Patsy, back at home with three small children, this wasn't part of the grand plan. The Patsy of those days needs to be defined by a man.

Man-Made Fibre evokes with wit and delight the lure of modernism, the shock of the new — and the way two (not so ordinary) human beings respond to the way things were, and the way things were going.

ISBN 0-7531-6875-8 (hb)
ISBN 0-7531-6876-6 (pb)

Astonishing Splashes of Colour

Clare Morrall

"A moving novel about loss, and particularly lost children" **Guardian**

Caught in an over-vivid world, Kitty feels haunted by her "child that never was". As children all around become emblems of hope, longing and grief, she begins to understand the reasons for her shaky sense of self.

What family mystery makes Kitty's four brothers so vague about her mother's life? And why does Dad splash paint on canvas rather than answer his daughter's questions? On the edges of her dreams, Kitty glimpses the kaleidoscope van that took her sister Dinah away — is it a link to her indistinct childhood?

ISBN 0-7531-7149-X (hb)
ISBN 0-7531-7150-3 (pb)